THE SECOND BASE CLUB

THE SECOND BASE CLUB

GREG TRINE

Henry Holt and Company
New York

Henry Holt and Company, LLC
Publishers since 1866
175 Fifth Avenue
New York, New York 10010
www.HenryHoltKids.com

Library of Congress Cataloging-in-Publication Data
Trine, Greg.
The second base club / Greg Trine.—1st ed.
p.   cm.
Summary: Sixteen-year-old Elroy will do almost anything, from joining
the wrestling team to forming a band, in order to get a girlfriend, but he
finally realizes the truth of a girlfriend's words about being himself.
ISBN 978-0-8050-8967-7
[1. Self-actualization (Psychology)—Fiction.   2. Dating (Social
customs)—Fiction.   3. High schools—Fiction.   4. Schools—Fiction.
5. Family life—California—Fiction.   6. California—Fiction.]   I. Title.
PZ7.T7356His 2010   [Fic]—dc22   2009050767

First Edition—2010/Book designed by Patrick Collins
Printed in the United States of America

1 3 5 7 9 10 8 6 4 2

To my brother Denny

THE SECOND BASE CLUB

Chapter One

I know it's not polite to stare at a girl's chest, but she was wearing one of those tops that said "Hey, stare at my chest, and do it now!" So I did. After all, I'd been given an order—a nonverbal one, but, still, an order was an order.

After she passed by, I wrote something down, then turned to my good friend Vern Zuckman. We had just gotten off work at Perry's Pretzels and were now sitting on a bench at the far end of the food court at the mall, trying to make the last day of summer last.

"I gave her an 8.65," I told him. "I had her in the mid-nines until I saw her face."

Vern snorted. "You're crazy, Elroy. She was a 9.8 easy. Didn't you see—" He stopped and looked at me. "Wait, you looked at her face?"

That was the difference between Vern and me. I saw the whole package. He only saw parts. Two in particular.

"I want one," he said.

"Sorry, pal. They come in pairs."

"I mean I want a girlfriend."

That made two of us.

It's not like I was completely without experience. Over the summer I'd made out with Jenny Brockmire three times. Twice for about thirty seconds, but one kiss lasted more than four minutes. She broke up with me when she realized I was timing her. She opened her eyes and saw me staring at the clock on the wall above the deep-fryer.

"Four minutes and twenty-one seconds," I told her.

She was not at all amused.

It was a little tense after that, and I ended up quitting Denise's Donuts and moving down to the far end of the food court, on the other side of Mario's Pizza-by-the-Slice, to Perry's. As far as I knew, Vern hadn't had any makeout experiences, but we were both of the same mind as far as girls were concerned. Tenth grade was about to begin. We'd be driving before the year was out. Something told me there was romance in our futures. It was time to get serious.

I pulled off my clip-on bow tie, the required uniform at Perry's, and shoved it in my shirt pocket along with the little notepad where I'd scribbled the 8.65. Turns out she was the highlight of the day. The three previous girls were in the mid-sixes—mid-sevens for Vern. But, like I said, he didn't rate the whole package.

"Let's get out of here," I said.

Vern stood up and looked around, his tie and notebook already stowed. "Yeah, it's thinning out. See you tomorrow, Elroy."

"First day of school. Woo-hoo." I slapped him a high-five.

We went outside and got on our bikes and headed out. Vern waved at the corner, and I took off down Casitas Pass. I lived with my mother at the end of the road in a thirty-two-foot

Airstream set in among the oaks. It wasn't part of a trailer park, just a lone trailer back in the canyon. So I lived in a trailer, not in a trailer park. I liked the distinction, for some reason.

It was a place some mountain man might call home, and I didn't feel I needed to hang my head about it. I saw deer and coyotes right outside the window on a daily basis. You don't get that in a trailer park.

I coasted off the pavement onto the dirt lot in front of the Airstream and brought the kickstand down as the bike came to a stop. Then I went inside. Mom was lying there in the living room, which was also my bedroom, with her legs flat against the floor and her arms pushing her torso up.

"No offense, Mom, but that's the worst push-up I've ever seen," I told her.

"It's yoga, dear."

Then she put her butt up in the air, with her hands and feet on the floor.

"Okay, *that's* the worst push-up I've ever seen."

"It's. Yoga. Dear."

Yoga or not, it was still a pretty rotten push-up, but I kept my mouth shut about it.

I wasn't at all nervous about tenth grade. I'd survived my freshman year mainly by sticking with large groups of other kids— safety-in-numbers kind of thing. Sure, some of the ninth-graders got beat up or had their heads flushed in the boys' bathrooms, but I was left alone through sheer luck. Like when there's a shipwreck and the sharks pick off the survivors on the fringe. I just never put myself on the fringe, and it worked. They never got to me.

And now, as a tenth-grader, I no longer had to worry about being the youngest and scrawniest. There was easier prey.

On the first day of school, I woke up early when my mom turned on the water in the shower. I lay there on the couch in the living/dining room and stared at the ceiling for a while before I got up and threw on some clothes. Actually, I didn't just throw them on. It was a carefully selected wardrobe. Jeans, white T-shirt, sneakers. Simple, but carefully selected. And I hoped some girl, in the mid-sevens or better, noticed.

When Mom wandered in wearing her Grinch bathrobe, I was already halfway through a piece of toast, and equally far into the morning paper.

"I made coffee," I said, pointing with a jagged piece of rye.

"Thanks." She poured a cup and joined me at the table.

"Remember, you'll be with your father this weekend," she said as she grabbed the funnies. "Let me know if he's working a real job."

I nodded. "Real job" to my mother meant working for someone else. It also meant getting a regular paycheck. My parents separated over this very issue. Mom said Dad had chronic entrepreneurism, meaning he had the heart to be self-employed, just not the brain. His latest business venture had failed, just like the previous three.

Which is why we eventually lost the house.

Which is why my parents aren't together.

Which is why I live at the end of Casitas Pass, along with a bunch of deer . . . and a few coyotes.

But they had been separated for a year, and neither of them had said anything about making it permanent. I took this as a good sign. Things could change for the better. There was hope.

I finished my toast and looked up at my mom. She was the kind of lady who looked great even before she put herself together completely. And that's saying something, since I'm her kid talking.

"You working today?" I asked her.

She worked at a spa in Ojai, doing massage mostly. She also taught yoga—she can touch her toes and everything—and ran the front desk when they were in a pinch. She hadn't dated anyone since she and my dad split. I wasn't sure why. She had a look that I imagined most men would go for. Vern once rated her in the nines. I punched him for that comment. You don't rate your best friend's mom.

Then again, maybe she didn't date because of Dad. Another good sign.

"Gotta keep this palatial estate running." She stood up and poured herself a second cup. "Don't be late for school."

"Can I ask you something, Mom?"

"Of course."

I got to my feet and turned slowly, letting her see my carefully selected outfit. "Do you think I have some lady-killer in me?"

"I'd say you're loaded with it."

"Or at least full of it?"

"Maybe. But in a good way."

I took off on my bike down Casitas Pass, leaving behind the orange groves and avocado trees. Once near the Highmont Ridge Mall, I kept an eye peeled for Vern. We had an understanding that we'd hook up at around the same time and place each morning and ride in together. He'd had his head flushed a few times as a freshman before I filled him in on my theory about keeping away from the fringe. Ever since then, he'd stuck to me like glue.

I glanced up and down the street, searching for him. He wasn't around, and after a while I continued on alone. I was at the rack locking my bike when he showed up.

"Why didn't you wait for me?" he asked, out of breath.

"You snooze, you lose."

"Needed a little extra beauty sleep, is all. That girl we saw at the mall yesterday might go to school here. I have to be prepared."

"She ignored us yesterday. It probably won't be much different today. We're sophomores, Vern, second to the bottom of the totem pole. Girls like that go for the varsity quarterback type." I was no quarterback, but I'd been told by a certain female that very morning that I had a fair amount of lady-killer in me. Of course, the female in question also happened to be my mother, but you have to trust your parents' opinions. It goes along with respecting your elders.

Vern locked his bike, and we headed to class. I didn't see him again until first break. We sat on one of the concrete planters in the quad, where we spent most of the previous year, far away from the fringe.

"I saw her," Vern said.

"Who?"

"The 9.8 from the mall."

"Don't you mean the 8.65?"

"Okay, I'll give you that. I looked at her face this time."

"You're learning," I said. "So what's her name?"

"Can't remember. I was too dazzled to think straight."

I told him that his mission, should he choose to accept it, was to find out her name and report back. He said he would, but as it turned out, Miss 8.65, whom I may have underrated, parked herself across the aisle from me in fourth-period geometry. I tried not to stare. It wasn't easy.

She caught me looking a few times, but at least I was looking at her face, not anywhere else. I think she appreciated it, because she smiled, which elevated her cuteness status even more.

The next day, Vern, who chose to accept his mission, reported that her name was Marisa Caldwell. Of course, I already knew this. Don't get me wrong, I was dazzled too. But I paid attention when Mrs. Dumar took roll.

Marisa. I wrote her name down on the inside cover of my geometry book, then in half a dozen places during fifth and six periods that first day, so I wouldn't forget. There wasn't much chance I would, but I wanted to be sure. I don't remember much about what went on in fifth and sixth periods. Did I have homework from those classes? If I did, the assignment was in one ear, out the other, and slowly making its way into outer space. Vern had said it best: dazzled.

CHAPTER TWO

I spent the week trying to work up the courage to talk to Marisa. So far, I could only stare. But at least I didn't stare at her chest—not when she would notice, anyway. I'd been a teenager for a few years now—I had highly developed check-out skills.

On Friday, I headed over to my dad's studio apartment, where I'd be for the weekend. He met me at the door and extended his hand. "Hey, Elroy." He'd been doing the handshake thing ever since I hit thirteen, thinking I was too mature to be hugged. This is just a theory, but do you ever outgrow the need for hugging? I'm not sure that you do.

I put on my grown-up face, though, and gave his hand a manly squeeze. "Hey."

Dad named me after a character from some ancient sixties cartoon called *The Jetsons*. Father George, daughter Judy, Jane his wife, and his boy Elroy. I'm not sure how I feel about being named after a cartoon character.

But, getting back to Dad's apartment. . . . Like I said, it was a studio, everything in one room. He slept on a fold-out couch, which was in couch mode now, facing an enormous television, one of his first purchases after the split with Mom.

"How does pancakes for dinner sound?" he asked, opening the fridge.

"Perfect."

Breakfast was my favorite meal. Pancakes for the next seven meals sounded good to me. While Dad mixed up the batter, I walked over and checked out his whiteboard, where he usually jotted down his latest business schemes. When I wanted to find out what was going on in my dad's head, I just read his whiteboard. It was pretty telling, usually.

But this time there were no business plans. No entrepreneurial schemes, half cocked or otherwise. The whiteboard simply had three items listed.

> Get a haircut
> Get in shape
> Earn her respect

Dad saw me looking at it and erased it, then went back to his pancake batter and called over his shoulder. "So how's your mother doing?"

"Fine," I said.

Dad looked at me like he wanted some elaboration on the subject, so I added, "She's not dating anyone. That's a good sign."

"That is a good sign." He paused, then said, "Does she ever talk about me?" He waved the question away with a spatula. "Don't answer that. Let's eat."

A few minutes later, he flipped the pancakes onto plates and we sat down at the table. "Who says bachelors don't eat good."

"Exactly."

Halfway through my second pancake, I put my fork down and looked across the table at my father. He used to box when he was in college and his nose was still slightly off kilter. He also had an old scar slicing through one eyebrow. But other than those few battle wounds, he was in pretty good shape for a guy in his forties. "You know, Dad, Mom doesn't want much. Just a normal life. A husband who works a normal job, gets paid whatever, and comes home."

He nodded. "I'm working on that. How is she?"

"You asked that already." I could tell he didn't want to discuss his past failures, so I let it go. "She says I have some lady-killer in me."

"That reminds me, Elroy. Did we ever discuss the birds and the bees?"

"I don't think so," I said. "What would you like to know?"

The birds and the bees was currently my favorite subject. All through dinner and later, as Dad laid out the Scrabble game, I couldn't stop thinking of Marisa Caldwell. Finally, I had to ask the question that had been banging around in my head since I first laid eyes on her. "Do you believe in love at first sight, Dad?"

Dad was arranging his letters and looked up. "Is that a hypothetical question?"

"Kind of." I mean, I did have a girl in mind, and I did feel something at first sight. Maybe it was just good ol' American horniness. Still, I was curious. Did love at first sight exist? Or did it just make for good storytelling?

"I believe in attraction at first sight." He laid down his letters, spelling GROUP on a double-word score. "Attraction at first sight happens all the time, which can grow into love. Generally, it's not love unless you know the person. That's the short answer, Elroy."

"What's the long answer?"

"The long answer is, it's complicated."

Actually, his long answer was shorter than his short answer. But I didn't say anything more. I had enough to go on. I wasn't in love with Marisa Caldwell—yet.

"So what's her name?"

"Huh?" I was busy fantasizing about Marisa and trying to come up with a word starting with "p." He wanted me to talk too?

"The girl's name," Dad said again.

"Marisa. But that's all I'm saying for now."

Dad didn't press for more information. He never did.

We got along fine over the weekend. He asked a lot about my mother, which was usual for him, but most of the time we just sat around watching manly movies and sports shows, playing Scrabble, and eating breakfast three times a day.

Back at school, I tried to keep myself from staring at Marisa Caldwell. She caught me looking a few times, but, like I said, I was looking in the right place, so I didn't have to blush. I blushed anyway. I think she just had that effect on guys. It couldn't be helped. She looked my way—I blushed.

I knew I'd have to speak to her eventually but didn't know what to say. Finally, near the end of the second week of school, I looked across the aisle and whispered, "Hey, Marisa, can I borrow a piece of paper?" In my head I kept chanting, *Keep eye contact. Don't look anywhere else. . . . Eye contact. . . . Eye contact.* My eyes obeyed, I think.

Marisa looked at me a long while before speaking. Then she said, "I take it that paper there is not in working order?" She gestured to my ring binder, where I had at least two hundred sheets of brand-new, unused paper. It was the beginning of the school year, for crying out loud. Who runs out of paper that fast?

I grabbed the top ring of the binder and gave it a fake tug while grimacing. "It's jammed. Won't open." Smooth.

When I turned back to her, she was holding a piece of paper across the aisle to me and smiling. I grabbed the paper, told her thanks, and got to work on the problems Mrs. Dumar had passed around. But Marisa's smile stayed with me, hovering over my page, right next to an isosceles triangle. I spent the rest of the period doodling, too distracted to tackle the Pythagorean theorem. At least I had broken the ice, I kept telling myself. I'd opened my mouth and spoken to Marisa Caldwell.

"You talked to her?" Vern unlocked his bike and looked at me with a combination of awe and disgust. "What happened to 'Girls like that go for the varsity quarterback type'?"

"Thought I'd aim high."

Vern said he wouldn't get in the way.

"That is so good of you," I said, and we both laughed. It wasn't like he was going to strike up a conversation with Marisa Caldwell anytime soon. But, in a way, I'd issued a challenge. I'd broken the ice with someone. Now it was his turn.

We rode home along the usual route, splitting up at the mall, and I headed down Casitas Pass. Mom wasn't around when I got there. Just me, the deer, and the coyotes. I threw my backpack on the living-room couch (my bed) and went outside again. If I was going to woo Marisa Caldwell, I'd better start by adding some muscle to my skinny frame. I picked out an oak tree with a branch about seven feet off the ground and did a few pull-ups— six, to be exact. But it was a start. I'd wait a few days, then go for seven, and maybe throw in some push-ups here and there. I know, it was kind of a vague workout plan, but it was a step in the right direction.

I worked at Perry's most of the weekend, along with Vern. Not much went on. We worked, got off, then sat on a bench and rated the girls going by. Nothing out of the ordinary, although we did see a few eights.

Monday, at school, Vern said, "What do you think that's all about?" He pointed to the far end of the quad, where the football team usually hung out. But instead of being just football players, the group was mixed. All of them were jocks, but not all of them were from the same sport. And the football team at Highmont was notorious for not fraternizing with nonfootball athletes.

"Not sure," I said.

There were a few swimmers, three baseball players, a gymnast, and a tennis player—even Todd Waylan, the best wrestler in the school, all rubbing elbows with the varsity football players. A lot of high-fives and laughter. Something was going on.

"We need to keep an eye on this . . . situation," Vern said.

"What situation? Maybe they're just enlightened. Accepting others is a good thing." I was joking. Last year, when Vern got his head flushed, it was the football team doing the flushing.

"The football team, enlightened? That would be a miracle," Vern said. "There's no such thing as a miracle."

Chapter Three

Seven and a half pull-ups. Thirty-two push-ups. Nineteen sit-ups. I was looking good. Sore, but looking good. Actually, I didn't notice a difference yet, it being only a few days into my workout regimen, but I felt more muscular, even if the world could not yet tell. And even if it wasn't exactly a regimen.

It had been a couple of days since I talked to Marisa, and I didn't want to wait too long before I did it again. I'd lose my momentum and have to start over. I had asked her for paper, and she had smiled. Maybe you didn't have to be the varsity quarterback to get to second base with her.

To be honest, I was a little vague on the whole bases thing. I was pretty sure I'd been to first before. Making out with Jenny Brockmire had to be first base. And I had a good idea what a home run was. But I was a little confused about what went on in the middle. What did second and third base mean, exactly? And would I have the guts to go there?

I didn't know. I just knew that I had to speak up in the very near future if I was going to have a chance to find out. I found my opening when Mrs. Dumar handed back our quizzes.

I'd scored a 93 percent. Looking across the aisle, I noticed that Marisa had a big fat "75" on the top of her paper. Obviously, she needed help. Maybe a tutor or something. A fellow student lending a hand. I put my paper on the edge of my desk, in plain view, then looked over at her.

"How'd you do, Marisa?"

She held up her paper, kind of embarrassed. "Starting off with a bang here."

I nodded. In my head I went through a dozen possible phrases to keep the conversation going: *Need some help? My tutoring services are available. Have you ever made out for more than four minutes and twenty-one seconds?*

I settled for short and sweet. "That sucks."

"Tell me about it."

It was the chance I'd been waiting for. She came right out and asked me to tell her something. I showed her my paper. "We should study together. I'm pretty good at math."

She went silent on me. Damn! I was too obvious. She was going to laugh.

The silence went on and on. Maybe I should take it back, just smile and tell her I was joking. But before I could get the words out, she beat me to it.

"Yeah, Elroy, that would be great. I need help, and you've got the brain power."

"I can't believe you," Vern said later that day, as we unlocked our bikes and headed home.

"What do you mean? Why would I lie?"

"I mean, it's great, but I still can't believe it. First asking for a piece of paper, and now you're her tutor."

"Yep. If all goes well, I'll have a date for Homecoming."

Homecoming was a pretty big deal at Highmont Ridge. Part of it was that our football team was nationally ranked, and one of our players, Sampson Teague, was an All-American. He played quarterback. Sportswriters were calling him the best thing to come out of California since John Elway. Not too shabby, since Elway was now in the Pro Football Hall of Fame.

So Homecoming was no small affair, and I had connections, if all went as planned with Marisa.

I didn't sleep much that night, partly because I had Marisa on my mind, and partly because I did a gazillion push-ups before I went to bed. Kind of hard to wind down after that.

The next day, I wore a tighter shirt than normal, in case my pecs wanted to show themselves. They hadn't in the past, but you never know. Then I sat in geometry, not exactly sure how to proceed. Marisa had agreed that she needed help and that I was the one to do the helping. Why was this so difficult? We'd had two conversations. I had to go for a third. But maybe she'd back out. Maybe she found someone smarter. Maybe—

The bell rang while I was maybe-ing myself to death, and I suddenly realized that Marisa had gathered her books and was now standing beside me. I looked up. Wow. She was still hot, even from new and unusual angles.

"So," she began, "another quiz on Friday. Did you mean it when you said you'd help me?"

"Absolutely." I grabbed my books and stood up. We were about the same height. She had a single curl of light-brown hair hanging along the side of her face. I had the sudden urge to yank on it, see if her bangs would part. Instead, I asked, "So—are you a study-at-the-library type, or do you do better at home?"

She pulled out a little scrap of paper and wrote on it. "Here's my address and cell-phone number. Why don't you come over around four."

I looked at the address. She lived on the hill above the junior college. Cute *and* rich. It occurred to me that she was out of my league. After all, I lived in a trailer in a canyon. I forced myself not to think about it.

"I'll be there."

"Don't do anything I wouldn't do," Vern said as we rode home.

I wasn't sure what he wouldn't do—or what he'd done, for that matter. But I decided I wasn't going to rush things. Seemed like a good plan. If she wanted to be more than student/tutor, I'd make sure my lips were in the vicinity.

I went home, had a snack, then headed to Marisa's house around three-thirty. The junior college wasn't far away, but I was traveling by bike. I needed the extra time, and I didn't want to arrive sweaty and gross. If I got there early, I'd circle the block a few times.

Her place stood near the end of a cul-de-sac, one of the biggest houses on the street. I did get there a little early, so I circled for a while in the street, until she opened the front door and waved me over.

"What are you waiting for?" she asked.

I pulled out my cell phone and looked at it. "It's not four yet. Thought I'd cram in a little exercise."

She laughed.

I parked my bike and walked up to her. She had changed into shorts and a tank top. Okay, yes, I looked at her chest for once. I don't know if it was just seeing her outside of school or what, but she looked hotter than normal, and I couldn't help wondering where we'd be studying—the dining room, on the back patio, her—*gulp*—bedroom?

Marisa seemed totally at ease, though, which made me realize she had nothing on her mind but math. I followed her inside and closed the door behind me. The floor was some kind of black-and-white marble. I looked around at the curved staircase, the massive portrait of her family on the far wall. Her father looked a little chubby, but her mom was a forty-something version of herself. Hot with a few more wrinkles. Marisa also had what looked like a little brother and a cat.

A chandelier hung above us. I had visions of its crashing down on me for thinking about sex when I should be thinking of math. And that's when I smelled it. Popcorn. We went into the dining room, where there was a table that could easily seat twenty people, a far cry from my table for four back home in the Airstream. Her math book lay opened to the proper page, and right next to it was a gigantic bowl of popcorn.

I grabbed a handful, stuffed my mouth, and mumbled, "You really know the way to a man's heart." Or a boy's, for that matter.

"I love popcorn," she said. Then she sat down and motioned me to the chair beside her. "Shall we?"

"Sure." I sat and grabbed a pencil. "May as well get our homework out of the way first."

She agreed, and we began working. I don't mind saying I was distracted. Guys like me are not used to girls like Marisa giving us the time of day. Even though I knew I was just there to teach, I kept thinking that if I was totally repulsive to her she wouldn't have invited me. Which meant there was hope.

But, like I said, I was distracted. At one point she let her knee rest against mine. My first impulse was to flinch and pull back, but I kept it there just to see if she realized our bodies were touching. Our bodies were touching!

"Are you okay?" she asked after a while. "I mean, you're sweating."

Was I okay? I wasn't sure. Part of me said, Yes, I'm much better than okay. I was hanging out with the prettiest girl in school. The other part of me said, Don't make more of it than it is, big guy. You're a tutor, nothing more.

I dabbed my face with my sleeve and said, "Sorry, math makes me sweat." Also, were you aware that our knees are touching? "My brain isn't used to working."

"Yeah, right."

We finished our homework and started doing some extra problems. Congruent triangles. Side-angle-side. Protractors and compasses. Before we knew it, it was six o'clock. The popcorn was gone, and it was time to leave.

"Thanks, Elroy," Marisa said as we headed for the door. "You're a good guy."

"I had fun. Math is easy, once you know the rules."

"Same time tomorrow?"

Whoa. She wanted to see me again! Maybe just to do math, but still.

"Sure."

I stood there for a few seconds, lingering, in case she gave me her makeout face. Or in case her lips did anything resembling a pucker. Nope . . . nothing. I turned around, jumped off her porch, grabbed my bike, and took off.

I couldn't help smiling. We'd worked on some math, shared a meal, and gotten to know each other a little better. Dad had said it wasn't love unless you know the person. I was on my way.

CHAPTER FOUR

O kay, her knee was bare, and I had on long pants. We didn't actually touch, not skin to skin anyway. Still, I'll never wash that knee again, I thought as I rode away from Marisa's house. Even though I'd made out a few times with Jenny Brockmire, knee touching with Marisa was more exciting. I guess it all depends on the girl and how much you like her. And I liked Marisa. She was more than just a pretty face—along with other attractive areas. She was interesting, friendly . . . and she told me I was a good guy.

I kept repeating her words as I pedaled down the street. "You're a good guy." Which could be interpreted as: *Want to make out? Want to be my boyfriend? What's your policy on slumber parties?*

When I reached the Highmont Ridge Mall, I pulled into the parking lot. I had to celebrate—not just that Marisa and I had touched knees, but that the whole situation had potential.

I locked my bike to a pole outside the food-court area and went inside. The place was fairly crowded. I ordered an iced mocha at Jake's Coffee Hut, found a vacant table, sat down, and checked out my surroundings. For some reason, I was in no mood to rate girls, and Vern wasn't around, which generally made it less fun. No one to compare tastes with. A bunch of ladies pushing strollers meandered here and there. Elderly couples were scattered throughout, sitting at tables. Laughter and conversations echoed off the high ceilings.

Some laughter rose above the rest, and a couple of voices sounded familiar. I scanned until I found them. Sampson Teague was there, surrounded by his minions. About eight or nine of them were seated at a table at the far end of the food court, and once again it wasn't just football jocks. A couple of baseball players, a swimmer, and a track star were included in the mix. What was going on?

I decided it was time to find out. I stood up and headed in their direction. They were too into themselves, and whatever they were up to, to notice me. I was glad to be anonymous. I'd never had my head flushed, but I wouldn't put it past them to try.

The table next to them was empty. I grabbed a chair and sat down. Though I was facing away, I was all ears.

"Quiet, guys," Sampson Teague was saying. He hit the tabletop with what sounded like an empty soda cup. "The Second Base Club is called to order."

Second Base Club?

A few people snickered. Someone said, "Personally, I'm going for a home run."

The cup hit the table again. "Yes, of course, Jerry, a homer is the ultimate goal," Sampson said. "But we have to call ourselves something. Now, listen up, guys. The point system goes like this. One point for second base, two points for third, and five points for a home run."

"Lady-killers unite."

Everyone laughed.

So that was it. They were keeping track. I wondered where touching knees would rate on their scale. Probably a bunt and getting thrown out at first.

I finished my mocha and went back outside. I didn't want to overstay my welcome. Didn't want to be recognized. You know what they say: Curiosity flushed the sophomore. As I was bending down to unlock my bike, I noticed a sign at Ernesto's Fine Mexican Food—*Help Wanted*. Come to think of it, Perry's Pretzels was getting a little old. And didn't you get tips working in a restaurant? And didn't I have a potential girlfriend? And didn't dating someone cost money?

You could enter Ernesto's from inside the mall or from the parking lot. I didn't want to face the Second Base Club. I walked over to a car and used the side mirror to check my teeth for any pieces of popcorn stuck between them. Then I shoved my hair to one side and went inside. It took a few seconds for my eyes to adjust to the dim light. When they did, I walked up to the hostess. She was dressed like some kind of Mexican peasant girl, with a white shirt that hung off one shoulder and a skirt that reached just past her knees. It was a pretty nice look, if you were into hot Mexican peasant girls.

"I saw the sign outside," I said, jabbing a thumb over my shoulder. "I'd like to apply for the job, if that's okay."

"Of course. You're the first one." She grabbed an application and handed it to me along with a pen, throwing me a pretty terrific smile.

Don't get distracted, Elroy, I told myself. You already have a potential girlfriend.

I filled out the application and handed it back to her.

"The general manager isn't here right now, but I'll pass this along. It's not a bad place to work. I'll keep my fingers crossed for you." Then she laid one of her smiles on me again.

I fumbled for something to say. When a girl smiles at you, it's important to say something witty or charming, possibly humorous. "Uh . . . I won't have to dress like a peasant girl, will I?"

She laughed. "No, only if you want to."

"Good. I think I'll pass."

"That would be my advice. I'm Juana Maria, by the way."

"Elroy. I'll keep my fingers crossed too."

I told her good-bye and went outside. But I have to say, her smile kind of stuck with me. Maybe I had a thing for Mexican peasant girls and didn't even know it.

The sun was going down, and it was cool on the ride up Casitas Pass. It felt like fall, finally. I pulled to a stop next to the Airstream. Mom was home, doing something at the stove when I went inside. It smelled good, whatever it was. My knee was completely back to normal; time to start thinking about my stomach.

"It's after seven," she said.

"Sorry, I was helping a fellow student with math." I plopped myself down on the couch and picked up my guitar.

"Fellow student?"

"Yep." I started in on "Stairway to Heaven." "An FFS." Speaking in code was always a good idea when dealing with a probing parent.

Mom stopped stirring and looked up. "FFS?"

"A female fellow student," I said, giving her my that's-all-you're-going-to-get-out-of-me look.

But her I'm-going-to-get-it-out-of-you-if-it-kills-me look had a little more power. My secrets were doomed.

"Okay, you have my attention. We can talk over dinner." She spooned some kind of rice-and-chicken concoction onto plates and placed them on the table. I sat down and she sat across from me, leaned on her elbows, and said, "Now, tell me everything."

There wasn't much to tell. I'd had a few conversations with a beautiful girl and we'd touched knees. I explained this to my mother, but the whole time I talked she kept searching my eyes for any hidden meaning.

I pretty much poker-faced myself through the entire meal. When in doubt, keep your parents in the dark.

"You can knock off the eyeball stare, Mom," I said finally.

"What do you mean? Haven't you heard? Eye contact is a good thing."

"Feels like you're trying to read the back of my skull."

She leaned a little closer. "Anything in there worth reading?"

"I'll let you know."

I stood up, grabbed my plate and hers, and put them in the dishwasher. Then I went to my room—meaning I crossed the room—and started on homework.

Mom just sat there at the table. I know she wanted more information, but I didn't have much to share. Not yet, anyway.

CHAPTER FIVE

All I needed was a little confidence. I'd already been told I was a good guy. I'd already touched body parts with the hottest girl I knew. Things were moving in the right direction, but how exactly does one increase his confidence?

The answer to that, I figured, was experience. Good old-fashioned romantic experience. Knee touching just wasn't going to cut it.

Vern and I went to the football game on Friday. I wasn't a raging Sampson Teague fan like the rest of the school (and town), but most of the girls would be at the game, including Marisa, and if I saw her now and then apart from math, maybe she'd begin to think of me as more than just another genius.

The key, I decided, was to show up to the game prepared, meaning I'd done tons of push-ups and as many pull-ups as I could. I had worked my way up to eight. So far the pecs hadn't decided to show themselves, but I remained hopeful.

We got to the stadium during the second half of the JV game and took a seat. The home-team side of the Highmont Ridge bleachers was built into the hillside. Vern and I sat near the top, which was a pretty good place to see the game, and an even better place to watch people. I began searching for Marisa. Vern scanned for anyone else, since we had an unspoken hands-off-Marisa agreement. Not that my hands were *on* her. That was another thing I was hopeful for.

The JV game ended, and when the varsity team took the field, everyone in the stands cheered, me included. I couldn't help it. I was caught up in the moment. Vern and I stood up with the crowd, clapping and cheering. We looked over at each other and shrugged.

"We're such sheep," I told him.

"I know."

When the game started, I got back to business, trying to spot Marisa. But the place was so crowded, it was difficult to find individual faces. Everything was a blur. There was only one thing to do—wander around and hope for the best. Or at least make frequent trips to the snack bar.

We did both. We wandered. We snacked.

Halfway through the second period, I spotted her standing with another girl. I searched my brain for something witty or charming or funny to say. I came up empty. I looked over at Vern, hoping he'd been struck by inspiration. He had three-quarters of a hot dog hanging out of his mouth. It was up to me.

Marisa spotted me and walked over along with her friend. I racked my brain. *Think, Elroy.* I tried to read her expression, but she was too busy trying to read mine. How can a girl give you a blank stare and look completely hot doing it? I decided to open my mouth and say whatever popped into my head, hoping something intelligent came out.

"Got any parallelograms on you?"

Lame!

Marisa turned to her friend, then turned back with the same blank expression.

"Hi, Elroy," she said after a while.

Whew!

Fortunately, Vern had swallowed by now, so his mouth was available for conversation. "Just say hi," he whispered. When I didn't, he jumped in. "Hi, Marisa, I'm Vern. You know my tongue-tied companion here, Elroy."

She laughed. So did her friend, which loosened things up a bit, and I found my voice. "How are you, Marisa?"

"Fine. This is Stacy."

Stacy was dark-haired and -eyed, and I suddenly flashed on the Mexican peasant girl Juana Maria over at Ernesto's. Life was getting more complicated by the minute.

We ended up sitting with Marisa and Stacy for the rest of the game. Vern was amazing. He was comfortable, confident. He told jokes I'd never heard before and kept the girls laughing. And I reaped the benefits. I was sitting next to Marisa in a non-math situation. Good ol' Vern.

The football game progressed. And Sampson Teague was his normal amazing self. He might be the big freshman-flusher on campus and the founding member of the Second Base Club, but I had to admire what he did on the field. Passing, scrambling, he could do it all. Highmont Ridge was kicking a little butt, to put it mildly.

But there was a problem. How to extend the evening? Vern

and I had come on bikes. We couldn't exactly ask the girls to climb on the back while we went for pizza or hamburgers.

When the girls got up to use the bathroom, I said, "Now what, Vern?"

"What do you mean?"

"I mean this is working. What do we do after the game?"

"You worry too much, Elroy. Haven't you ever heard of going with the flow?"

"I've heard of that," I said. But I wasn't sure if it ever worked. Especially when you're trying to gain some ground in the guy/girl department. "Describe the go-with-the-flow technique again?"

"Marisa and Stacy know that we don't have cars. All that matters is that they're having a good time, and I think they are."

Sampson Teague connected on a twenty-yard pass into the end zone, and the crowd erupted. For some reason, I kept waiting for the instant replay. When the cheering died down, I turned to Vern. "Yeah, the girls are having a good time, I think. All that laughter has to mean something. How'd you become so funny all of a sudden?"

Vern shrugged. "I have no idea." He took a swig of Coke. "Here they come, Elroy. Remember, go with the flow. If we don't hook up tonight, we can arrange something for later. All that matters is that they have a good time here and now."

It was a pretty vague plan, but it was all we had for the moment. I tried to place myself in go-with-the-flow mode. For starters, I put a smile on my face. Then, when the girls sat back down, I said the first thing that popped into my head.

"So—did you miss us?"

"We did," Marisa said.

"Yeah, you should have seen us in the bathroom pining away," Stacy added and laughed.

Laughter is good, I thought. You can't laugh and not be enjoying yourself, right?

So we sat there together and watched the game. The four of us. And the more I sat there, the more natural it felt. Halfway through the third quarter, I realized I was thigh to thigh with Marisa. Thigh to thigh! Which is way better than knee to knee. Things were moving in the right direction. I better start getting my lips prepared, I told myself. Just in case, because you never know.

Marisa said, "What are you guys doing after the game?"

Vern and I exchanged a look, probably thinking the same thing: *We came on bikes. Now what?*

Vern had the right idea. Stall. "What did you have in mind?"

"I mean, do you have to get home right away?" Marisa asked.

"Not me," Vern said. "You, Elroy?"

I shook my head. "Nah. No worries. My parents don't care how late I stay out." I don't know why I said "parents," as if I lived with both of them. On the other hand, I was pretty sure my mother wasn't expecting me immediately after the game. And she did want more details about my romantic life. How could I give her details if I never experienced anything?

"Wanna hang out?" Stacy said.

Wow. This going-with-the-flow stuff really worked. I thought I saw Vern salivating, and I almost forgot that I was thigh to thigh with Marisa or that there was a football game going on.

It was the crowd that brought me back. Apparently, Sampson Teague had connected with another pass into the end zone. I glanced up at the scoreboard. We were ahead 42 to 13, four minutes left in the game. Good, this thing was almost over. Time for some serious flirting.

"You guys like pizza?" Marisa asked.

Actually, I was stuffed from all our trips to the snack bar, but I just nodded and made myself look as hungry as possible. Vern had the same look. We both nodded, and I said, "I'd kill for a slice of pepperoni." Fortunately, Santino's Pizza was about a block from school. I thought of asking Marisa if she'd like to ride on the handlebars of my bike, but decided against it. We'd walk. More time for conversation, and better on the ass.

After the game, we followed the crowd out of the stadium. Turns out, Santino's was the place to be. A bunch of cheerleaders were already there, sitting at an enormous table near the back, obviously getting ready for a large group. I also saw a few familiar faces here and there, and a handful of parents wearing Highmont Ridge sweatshirts. We grabbed a booth off to one side and ordered drinks while we decided what kind of pizza to get.

"Don't look now," Vern said, nodding toward the door, "but God just showed up."

I glanced over my shoulder, and there he was, Sampson Teague and a half-dozen of his football cronies, coming through the front door. A few people clapped. Some cheered. A parent slapped Sampson on the back. Another shook his hand. Then he headed for the table with the cheerleaders.

At one point, Marisa got up to go to the bathroom, and Sampson Teague's mouth dropped open like a drawbridge as he watched her cross the room. When she came back, his eyes followed her to our table. Then he gave me a look like he wanted to score and I was the linebacker in his way.

CHAPTER SIX

She hugged me. Marisa Caldwell hugged me. A real one too. Not one of those A-frame kinds, where you and the other person bend at the waist so that just your shoulders touch, followed by a rapid pat on the back. This was a real hug—her body pressed up against mine.

Knee to knee, thigh to thigh, and now chest to chest. Or, even better, chest to breast!

This was how the football/pizza evening ended, with Marisa wrapping her arms around me. Vern and Stacy shook hands, I think.

When I got home, Mom was in her bedroom watching TV.

"How'd it go?" she called to me, muting the sound.

I walked down the hall and poked my head in through the doorway. "Great. Vern and I went to pizza after the game. Had a good time."

She was doing the read-the-back-of-my-skull thing again, but I tried to ignore it. I didn't have anything more to share, and

I was pretty sure there was nothing visible on the back of my skull. I told my mother good night, and went back to the living room. I lay there in the dark for a long time, replaying it all in my head. Everything was moving in the right direction. Now, if I could just keep the momentum going. . . .

During the school day, Marisa and I still didn't hang out. We were kind of friends. We hung out at football games (game) and went to pizza places (place) together. But for some reason we weren't at the point where I'd sit with her group during lunch or she'd sit with mine. Not sure why.

Monday, after school, we met again at her house for more math and popcorn. It's funny how knee touching no longer did it for me. I kept inching my chair closer to hers, until she looked at me funny and I decided to cool it. Just concentrate on math, I told myself.

"You're sweating again," she said more than once. "Want me to open a window?"

I shook my head. "Brain workout. Does it to me every time."

Tuesday was more of the same. So was Wednesday.

And that's when it hit me—one of us was going to have to make a move. One of us was going to have to risk something if we were ever going to be more than tutor/student with the occasional football game and pizza thrown in. I wanted more than football and pizza. The question was, did she? What was going on in that fantastic-looking head of hers?

Take a risk, Elroy, I told myself.

And so, on Friday, I did. I lingered after the math session. Most of the houses in Marisa's neighborhood had porches, and hers had a swing.

"Uh . . . I don't have to get home right away." I looked over at the porch swing. "Want to give that thing a whirl?" I wasn't sure if you could actually whirl on a porch swing, but you get the idea. Linger . . . see where it leads.

Porch swings are pretty darn romantic, I decided. Sitting there, thigh to thigh with the girl of your dreams, the tips of your toes touching the ground just enough to keep the thing in motion.

It was dark out, and I could see an old guy across the street sitting on his porch, smoking a cigar and watching us. His sprinklers were on and were doing a good job watering the street. Take the risk, Elroy.

I swallowed hard as my heart hammered inside me. Then I reached over and took Marisa's hand in mine. In the next few seconds, this relationship would be over or we'd be at another level. She'd bolt or she wouldn't. There was no middle ground.

She didn't bolt. She stayed. And her hand was kind of clammy. Maybe she was as nervous as I was. I looked across the street and saw that the old geezer was still watching. I wished he'd go inside. I waited several minutes, hoping he'd pick up the mental telepathy I was sending his way. It didn't work, and so I turned to Marisa and tried to plant one on her.

An overhead light came on, bathing us in five hundred watts of white light.

"Motion sensor," Marisa said. "No sudden movements."

We sat there motionless for about five minutes, waiting for the darn thing to turn off. Meanwhile, Old Man Cigar was looking at us and smiling—clearly, this was better than *Jeopardy!* He lit another cigar and settled in for the evening.

Finally, the light switched off again. I began turning my head toward Marisa in one-inch intervals. She smirked, knowing what

I was up to. She whispered, "Nothing sudden, now, Elroy. Slowly, very slowly."

It took me a couple of minutes to close the gap between us. And she didn't make it any easier by coming my way. "Wipe that smirk off your face and get those lips over here," I told her.

She leaned toward me, and I said, "Slowly, Marisa. I've worked hard to get this far."

Our lips met. And it was worth the wait. I tried not to count, but I couldn't help myself. We made it to nine seconds before I broke it off without moving too much.

"That bad, huh?" she said.

"You're not going to believe this, but I have an itch."

"Is that all? You had me worried."

We kissed again, and this time I didn't count. But my knee itched like crazy. When I couldn't take it anymore, I broke it off and reached for my knee. Immediately the light went on again, and from across the street I could hear the old man laughing.

While I debated how to unscrew the five-hundred-watt bulb without burning my fingers, Marisa's parents pulled up in the driveway. No chance of being alone now. Our evening was over.

Nine seconds, I told myself as I headed for home. The best nine seconds of my life.

CHAPTER SEVEN

My dad got a job working for Animal Control. He drove around in a big truck with lots of built-in cages in the back. Basically, he was one of Highmont Ridge's dogcatchers, but occasionally he had to deal with wayward possums or raccoons, and now and then a reptile.

"Do I look any taller to you?" he asked. We were at his place, sitting down to our usual dinner of pancakes.

I took a bite and looked up, cocking an eyebrow, since my mouth was full.

"Yeah, you heard right—taller. I had a close encounter with a boa constrictor. He put the squeeze on me. I was hoping to get a few inches in height out of it." He smirked.

I knew he was joking, but I went along with it. "Stand up and I'll let you know." When he did, I looked him over, then shook my head. "You look about the same to me. Your face is a little redder, though. That must have been some squeeze."

"It was." He sat back down. "So how are things at school?"

My mind flashed on Marisa and our brief moment on the porch. "It's going great." For some reason I was waiting for him to lock eyeballs with me and examine the back of my skull, but Dad wasn't into the intimidate-with-his-eyes thing. Instead, he simply asked direct questions.

"Tell me about the girl." See? He glanced up at the ceiling, thinking. "What was her name again? Marisa?"

"Yes."

"Well?"

"Well what?" I said.

"How about a little more information?" He laced his hands behind his head and waited. He didn't stare like Mom. He just waited, hoping I couldn't stand the silence. It was pretty effective. He began bouncing his biceps, alternating arms, keeping pace with a blaring stereo from a car passing by on the street.

I finally gave in. "I'm tutoring her in math, so we're hanging out, getting to know each other. I think."

"And you're wondering if it's love yet?"

"Well, it's not wearing off. If anything, I like her better now that we've had a few conversations. How soon before I know if it's love?"

Dad laughed. "Good question."

"And the answer is?"

"The answer is, I don't have the answer. Discovering the answers is what makes life worth living. Didn't I tell you that?"

"You're no help."

He dabbed at a spot of syrup and popped the last piece of pancake in his mouth. "You'll figure it out, Elroy. Scrabble?"

"What about the dishes?"

"Never do today what you can put off till tomorrow."

Sometimes my father was too wise for words. With regard to dishes, that is. His girl advice left something to be desired. I glanced at his whiteboard to see what else was going on in his head. In place of the usual list of goals, he'd drawn a rectangle.

I picked up the whiteboard and turned it around, in case there was anything on the back. It was blank. "Okay, I give up. What is it?"

"It is whatever I want it to be."

"So the board is blank because your mind is?"

"That's about the size of it. But something's brewing inside; I can feel it."

He got out the Scrabble game, and we played until midnight. After beating me twice, he said, "You're not completely here tonight, are you? Something on your mind?"

"Someone," I said.

"I figured." He went into pause mode again, his version of the Mom-stare. But it was getting late, I'd already shared all I wanted to, and the nine-second smooch was none of his business.

"Nine seconds is not much," Vern said as we rode to school on Monday.

"It would have gone on longer, but I had an itch." I thought for a second. "I think I'm giving up counting for Lent."

"It's October."

"I'm starting early."

All morning long, I thought it through. Were Marisa and I

boyfriend and girlfriend now? After all, things had been moving along. We touched knees, legs, chests, lips—in that order. But what exactly did this mean? Were we supposed to hang out at school now? Was I supposed to carry her books? Should we hold hands between classes?

Once again, it all came down to risk. If I wanted to find out where we stood, I'd have to be direct about it. Do or die, I told myself. Find out once and for all.

Between classes, I checked myself out in the bathroom mirror. Not too shabby. At least I hoped so. I licked my lips. I puckered. I was ready.

At first break, I spotted Marisa near her locker and walked over. "Hey, Marisa," I said. "How was your weekend?"

She turned to face me. "Fine. How's it going?"

Okay, the preliminaries were over. Time to move on. I leaned toward her with a slight pucker, eyelids at half mast.

She turned away. "Don't."

I stood there, leaning, my mouth slightly open. *Don't? Don't at school because everyone is looking? Or don't ever—as in "Hit the Road, Jack"?*

"Something wrong?" I asked.

"Sorry about Friday."

"What's to be sorry about?"

She looked away, avoiding my eyes. "I don't want you to get the wrong idea. I don't like you in that way."

What? She doesn't like me that way? "So what was all that hugging and kissing about?"

"All that hugging and kissing? One hug. One kiss."

Actually, it was two. We kissed, I commented on my itch, and we kissed again. Definitely two kisses.

Marisa closed her locker and turned to face me, and something inside started to ache. Neither of us spoke. We weren't exactly boyfriend and girlfriend, were we? So why did I care? Why did I feel like someone had just reached inside me and ripped out a piece? A vital piece.

I opened my mouth to say something. Nothing came out but air.

She shifted her weight from one foot to the other. "How can I put this, Elroy?"

I knew what she was going to say before she said it.

"I just want to be friends."

Friendship was a good thing, right? But it felt like I'd been stabbed with a jagged knife. Or kicked in the head.

People were walking by, rubbernecking. Was it that obvious? Did I have that *Just Dumped* look on my face? My stomach began to ache. Like someone had force-fed me a frozen bowling ball and it was growing colder by the second.

"What about the math tutoring?" I asked, forcing myself to ignore the pain.

"I guess we should give that a break. Thanks for the help. I mean that."

She walked away, and I stood there watching until she disappeared around the corner. Then I kept staring, as if she'd somehow magically appear and tell me she was kidding—an early April Fool's. Only she didn't come back, and I stood there staring at nothing as the hall emptied around me. I glanced at the locker in front of me and punched it as hard as I could. My knuckles split and began to bleed, but I didn't feel it.

I cut the rest of my classes. I couldn't bear the thought of anyone seeing me cry.

I didn't go to school the next day. When the phone rang, I didn't answer it. I lay in bed, staring at the ceiling, moaning, some gut-wrenching despairing noise rising from my soul. I found it hard to move. How could I go back to the same school, or, worse, the same math class? I kept the blinds down and slept way more than I needed to.

That afternoon, Vern showed up.

"Something wrong with your phone?" he asked when I came to the door.

He had on an Evel Knievel shirt, and his eyes were a bit watery from the long ride up Casitas Pass. He came inside and looked around. "The sun's up, big guy. Open a blind. Let some light in."

I flopped down on the bed/couch and let out the world's biggest sigh.

"So this has something to do with the girl?"

"She dumped me, Vern."

He sat down at the table. "How could she dump you? You weren't even going out. Come on, Elroy, it was just one kiss."

"It was two kisses!" I practically screamed. It was definitely two kisses. Why couldn't anyone get it right? Kiss . . . comment . . . kiss. Two.

"Okay, two kisses. Still, she was only a potential girlfriend, not a real one. And you know what that means?"

"No, Vern," I said in a bored voice. "Tell me what it means."

"It means you're not dumped."

I sat forward on the couch, thinking it over. Vern had a point. How can you be dumped by someone who was just a potential girlfriend? But knowing this didn't help. I still wasn't with Marisa.

"Ever had a stomachache for twenty-four hours, Vern?"

"Not one caused by a girl."

"It sucks."

"Can I load you up with some clichés?"

"Clichés?"

"Yeah. There's more fish in the sea. Every cloud has a silver lining. If you fall off the horse, you get back on. And my personal fave"—he drum-rolled on the edge of the table—"if at first you don't succeed . . ." He gestured at me to finish.

I wasn't in the mood.

"You're no fun. I'm telling you, clichés work wonders."

I ignored him. We sat in silence for some time. Vern grabbed a pencil and started working a crossword puzzle. I picked up my guitar and played the same chord over and over.

After a while, he tossed aside the crossword puzzle and looked at me. "Get that whipped look off your face, Elroy. I mean it."

I frowned. "How's this?"

"Better. We should go to the game on Friday, don't you think?"

I kept quiet. Going out in public was the last thing I wanted to do.

"Elroy? Football game on Friday, we're going, right?"

I said nothing.

"Okay, let me rephrase it. You're going to the football game on Friday. I'm telling you, not asking. You're going; it's a fact." When I didn't respond, he added, "Don't make me come over there."

"Okay," I said finally. "Let's go to the game on Friday." Frankly, I'd rather move into a cave, but I'd force myself to get out there. If nothing more than to show Marisa that I wasn't down for the count. It sure felt like I was, but she didn't have to know that.

My stomach hurt almost constantly, spiking during fourth-period math. I found a place to sit on the other side of the room, as far as I could get from Marisa without being in another classroom. It didn't help. I found myself constantly gazing across the room, looking for any hint of interest, as if it had all been a dream, as if she hadn't completely body-slammed me with the "just friends" line.

And then something happened to make it worse.

Vern and I were in our usual spot in the quad when Marisa walked by, hand in hand with Sampson Teague. I couldn't believe it. Not being with her was one thing. Seeing her with someone else took it to a new level.

Vern looked at me. "That was fast."

"Guess you were right, Vern," I said.

"I know I'm right, but in this instance what are you referring to?"

"She *is* the type to go after the quarterback."

For the rest of the week, it was the same. Whenever I saw Marisa, I saw Sampson, and vice versa. And when Marisa wasn't around, Sampson was hanging with the Second Base Club. I wondered if I should tell her about the secret organization and their even more secret agenda. Marisa was just another notch on his locker.

She needed to know the truth, I decided, but how to do it without sounding like the former jilted potential boyfriend? I slipped a note through the slats in her locker. It was the only way. Typed, in case she'd recognize my handwriting.

Marisa,

  Don't trust Sampson Teague. He's after one thing and one thing only. Ask him about the Second Base Club if you don't believe me.

A Friend

The rest was up to her.

CHAPTER EIGHT

I was surprised when I got the call from the Mexican restaurant where I had applied. It had been so long ago. Ernesto looked like an Ernesto, hair as black as tar and eyes almost as dark. The interview was quick: What times are you available? Do you play sports? Applicable work experience?

It was clear he needed someone; the interview was just a formality. I asked a few questions to sound interested. Finally, Ernesto reached across the desk and shook my hand. "Elroy, welcome aboard."

I thanked him and turned to leave.

"One more thing, Elroy."

"Yes?"

"You've met our hostess, right?"

I nodded. "Cute girl."

"She's my niece. I'm very tight with her father. Just so you know . . . he's a little crazy. And he's got a huge baseball bat."

I raised my hands with my palms out. "Hey, I'm just looking for a job."

"I'm just saying. I'd hate to see you get your knees broken when there are plenty of girls out there with normal fathers."

"I already have a girlfriend," I lied.

"Then your knees will be safe."

"Well? Are you in or out?" asked the Mexican peasant-girl hostess, not necessarily in that order. I'd put her at girl Mexican hostess peasant.

"I'm in." I walked past her, then turned around. "Juana Maria, right?"

"No buttering up your co-workers," she said and smiled.

"Do you remember my name?"

Her face dropped. "Elwood?"

"I love it when I make such a big impression on someone. It's Elroy."

"I knew there was an 'El' in there someplace. Do I get half-credit?"

"You do. See you later, Juana Maria."

"See you, Elwood."

"Elroy!"

Vern and I went to the game on Friday. I made a deal with Ernesto to keep my Fridays open at least until football season was over. He understood. A guy had to have a social life. After all, Highmont Ridge had a championship team. Of course, Vern and I weren't there to root them on. We were there to socialize, fraternize, flirt.

At least, Vern was there to flirt. It was all I could do to

remain upright. But I knew I needed this. If I was going to get back on that horse, I had to at least join the human race, even when every impulse told me to crawl beneath the nearest rock.

We arrived at the Highmont stadium just before the start of the varsity game. The captains from both teams were meeting with the referees for the coin toss at center field.

"Plenty of fish in *this* sea," Vern said, scanning the crowd. Highmont football was big enough news to attract people who didn't attend our school. And some of them were, of course, female. It was a bigger sea, which meant more fish.

"Let's find a seat," I suggested. "We'll wait until the line dies down before we hit the snack bar."

"Sounds like a plan."

It was a rout from the start. Sampson Teague kept the ball on the ground most of the time and passed just enough to keep the defense guessing. If Marisa was there, I didn't see her. Good. My stomach wasn't back to normal yet, but it was getting better. I didn't want to see her. Then again, I did. I can't explain it.

"What do you think?" Vern asked midway through the first period.

"About?"

"The girl hunt. You're Mr. Experience. My lips are still virgins."

"Really?" I guess I knew Vern didn't have much experience, but he'd never really come out and said it until now.

"Really. Now, what's the plan?"

The plan. I didn't know. My heart was still a train wreck. Kind of hard to think of jumping right back in. I knew I needed to, but knowing and doing were two different things. I hadn't thought it through any further than showing up at the football game and being our charming selves . . . or at least riding on Vern's charming coattails. But now that we were here and nothing was happening, it was clear that we had to step it up a notch and take some risks. Damn. Risk is what ended things with Marisa.

"Uh . . . eating sounds good," I said.

"That's the plan?"

"Yes, but eat with good table manners. You can't impress girls if you're a slob."

"That's the plan?" he said again.

"Follow me."

We headed to the snack bar, keeping our eyes peeled for someone cute. Preferably two someones. We ordered hot dogs and went over to the condiments table for mustard and relish.

"Heartache at three o'clock," Vern said, nodding to the right.

I turned and locked eyes with Marisa for a nanosecond before she turned away. More like stomach pain at three o'clock. She was with Stacy, who at least acknowledged Vern with a nod.

"Should I say something?" I asked Vern.

"It's your heart," he said. "I'm just the sidekick."

Marisa came closer, and all I could think about was how hot she looked. She was in jeans and a baggy sweatshirt, and completely beautiful.

"Your call, Elroy," Vern said. "I won't say hi unless you do."

But my mouth went totally dry. I moved my lips but nothing came out. Marisa passed us by and quickly disappeared into the crowd.

I looked down at my hot dog again and saw my hand squeezing the life out of the mustard bottle. My appetite was history.

"Wow, you really like mustard."

"Let's go," I told him.

Just when you think you're over a stomachache, it comes back with a vengeance. How could a potential girlfriend make a guy feel like that? Vern was right, we really weren't an item, just two almost friends who kissed for nine seconds. It was like she got a brief taste of me and spat me back out. I was saliva—a big fat Marisa loogey.

There was nothing to do but watch the game. I was no longer in the mood for even a halfhearted girl-hunt.

"Remember, you weren't dumped," Vern said.

"Just watch the game."

The rest of the game was kind of a blur. Highmont came out victorious. Touchdowns were scored, tackles were made, and my eyes saw it all. But my brain didn't process it. The lights were on . . . then again, they weren't.

Vern and I rode home on our bikes after the game. We parted ways at the mall. "Sorry I was such a basket case, Vern."

"You just need more time," he said. "But I expect you to be back to normal on Monday. If you're not"—he made a fist—"the wrath of Vern."

"I'll see what I can do."

I turned up Casitas Pass and headed for the sanctuary of the Airstream. Maybe some alone time with my guitar would put me right again. But somehow I knew it wouldn't. No amount of alone time could fix this.

I stopped in the middle of the road and turned my bike around. Maybe I was insane. Maybe I was losing my mind, but I couldn't help myself. I had to try one more time with Marisa. I couldn't let go until I did.

I rode back down Casitas Pass, pumping hard as I passed the avocado trees. After a while, I slowed down. No need to show up at Marisa's house out of breath and sweaty. This was my last chance; I needed to make a good impression.

I cruised by the mall, then headed up the hill above the junior college. It had to be close to eleven. What if Marisa was asleep? Maybe I'd made the trip for nothing. I turned onto her street and stopped, not sure if I could go through with it, not sure what I'd say.

My cell phone vibrated in my pocket. I answered it.

"Elroy?" It was my mother.

"Hi, Mom."

"Where are you? Are you all right?"

"Sorry, I should have called. Vern and I stopped to get something to eat." It wasn't a lie. We did get something to eat. And we stopped to do it. It just happened to be at the game.

"When are you coming home?"

"I'm on my way." Okay, that was a lie. "See you soon, Mom. Don't wait up."

"I always wait up. It's my job."

"I guess. See you in a few . . ." minutes if things went bad, hours if things went well.

I hung up and turned my attention back to the street. Marisa's house was about six doors down on the right. I pedaled slowly, gathering my nerve. Ten minutes from now, I'd know for sure. One way or another, it would be over or not over.

Marisa's place was completely dark. But the cigar-smoking old man was sitting on his porch across the street, watching nothing. As I got closer to her house, I noticed a car out in front. I stopped.

Suddenly the porch light came on. Motion detector. There she was, sitting on the porch swing, and she wasn't alone. Sampson Teague was right there beside her, both of them staring at me. I turned my bike around and got out of there as fast as I could.

And I could hear the old man—laughing.

I switched gears as I reached the end of her block and the street sloped down. Thighs pumping hard. Three blocks away now, and the old man's laughter stayed with me, locked inside my head. I raced on, paying little attention to intersections, even the ones with stop signs. My legs burned, but I didn't slow down, not until I ran the red light on Ashwood. Not until it was too late. Not until I heard the tires screech and the horn blare. I looked up just in time to see the truck sliding to a stop in front of me. I hit the driver's side at the front wheel, which stopped my bike but not me. I flew over the hood and kept going, hitting the ground on the other side, palms, knees, and chin slowing me down until the curb stopped me.

"You okay, kid?" It was the guy from the truck.

I got to my feet slowly. Very slowly, and trying to focus on the world spinning by.

"Kid, you okay?"

"I'm fine," I lied. My jeans were torn. So were my palms. My chin throbbed.

The man just stood there, looking at me like I was some kind of ghost. A bleeding one.

"I said I'm fine, okay!" I yelled. "Leave me alone!"

"Hey, man, take it easy." He got back in the truck and drove away.

I walked over to my bike, which was still in the middle of

Ashwood. The front wheel was bent nearly in half. I dragged it to the sidewalk, then grabbed my phone and dialed home.

"Mom, I wrecked my bike. Can you come and get me?" I couldn't keep my voice from cracking, but I held the tears off until I hung up.

CHAPTER NINE

"**I** don't need a doctor," I said, for about the millionth time. "I'm scraped up. Nothing's broken."

Mom was trying to keep her eyes on the road and check me out at the same time.

"You're sure?"

"I'm sure. Eyes on the road, Mom."

She nodded. A few minutes later, we were heading up Casitas Pass. "So tell me what happened."

"I ran a red light. I hit a truck."

"Not that story," she said. "Tell me the other story."

I folded my arms and leaned against the door. "I don't want to talk about it."

"That's not good enough, Elroy. Try again."

She had a point. But how much did she need to know? Certainly not everything.

I looked over and met her stare. "Mom, the road!" Then I

said, "I made a fool of myself tonight. That's all you need to know."

"I see," she said. "Over a girl, I take it?"

"Yes. Over a girl."

"We'll get you bandaged up and get you to bed. How's that sound?"

"Sounds like a plan."

The following day, I started work at Ernesto's. Juana Maria was my trainer.

"Hello, Elwood," she said. She had on her Mexican peasant-girl outfit again. I wore bell bottoms and a puffy white shirt.

"It's Elroy."

"I know." She grinned. "Hello, Elwood."

"Hi. Let's get this road on the show. What do I do?"

"Gee whiz. Don't you know how to fraternize? Remember, all work and no play makes Jack a dull boy."

I could see her eyeing the bandage on my chin, but she didn't ask about it, which was fine by me. I was done talking about my banged-up exterior and my bleeding insides.

"I thought I was Elwood."

"That's it. You're fraternizing! Now, Elroy, your job is to greet the customers, take down their names, and seat them when there is an available table."

"How complicated," I said.

"You'd be surprised. We also help clear tables when we can, make salads, fold napkins. It can get pretty busy on a weekend. You'll see."

Turned out, she wasn't lying. All night long it was tag-team hostessing—or hosting. I'd seat someone while she cleared a table, and vice versa. It didn't slow down until ten o'clock. We spent the remaining half-hour wrapping silverware in cloth napkins. Kind of like making burritos. I was getting it down. And I actually had a good time. Who knew work could be fun?

The following day, I bought a new front rim and tire for my bike.

On Monday, I met up with Vern at the mall and we rode to school together. He kept eyeing me strangely, like I had an enormous zit on my face. I was pretty sure I didn't. I check that kind of thing before I leave the house . . . trailer.

"What is it?" I asked.

"Just checking."

"Checking?"

"Trying to see if you're back to normal. Remember, the wrath of Vern. So how is it going?"

We stopped at a traffic light and I looked at him. Should I tell him about seeing Marisa and Sampson on the porch swing, about the old man laughing? I decided against it. "It's over," I said. "There's nothing I can do about it. How's that?"

I didn't mention that I still thought about her constantly and that the frozen bowling ball never got any smaller . . . or less cold.

"Dang. No wrath of Vern. I was looking forward to it."

We got to school and locked our bikes. I avoided all contact with Marisa. I knew where she'd be likely to hang out between classes, and I simply avoided those areas. But that didn't mean I didn't bump into Sampson.

Vern and I were dressing for sixth-period PE. Sharing the same locker room with football players had to be some form of cruel and unusual punishment.

"So what's the score?" I heard one of them say.

"I heard Sampson scored a home run over the weekend."

"That lying sack of you-know-what."

Vern shot me a look. I was about to say something when—

"Someone mention my name?" It was Sampson, the potential-girlfriend stealer himself. The members of the Second Base Club were grouped at the far end of the locker room, slapping high-fives and patting one another on the back.

"So is the rumor true, Sampson?" someone asked. "I heard you—"

I elbowed Vern. "Let's get out of here."

We went out onto the track and began jogging, which was the routine for sixth-period PE. Mr. Teitsort wasn't one of those hands-on instructors. He took roll, told us to run, then came out and told us to shower when class was over. That was about it.

But running felt good, for some reason.

"What do they have that we don't have?" I asked Vern.

"Abs? Pecs? Biceps? Is that what you mean?"

"I'm not sure," I said. "It just seems like guys who go out for sports do a little better in the girl department."

"You think?"

"Yes, I think. What sport can we go out for?"

"I'm not sure. Is there a bowling team?"

"I don't think so." Somehow I doubted bowling would qualify as a sport. And it certainly wouldn't impress a girl. Sweat had to be involved.

That night, I thought it over. Mom kept giving me the look that said she knew there was more to the drive-full-speed-into-a-truck story.

"I'm thinking of going out for a sport," I said as we were sitting down to dinner. "Any ideas what sport I can do?"

"You'd be excellent at yoga. Can you touch your toes?"

"I can touch my shins." I shook my head. Yoga wouldn't cut it. "I mean a team sport. Something at Highmont. What can I do?"

She didn't have any ideas besides yoga. She just told me what I already knew, that I'd never been a sports person, that I was years behind all the other kids in that area. And I wasn't exactly a big guy.

But there had to be something I could do, some sport where I could start out with no experience and where size didn't matter. I'd mull it over. I'd sleep on it.

The following day, it came to me during the all-school assembly. I found Vern in the gym, sitting next to Tuck Mayfield, a kid we'd known since fourth grade. Tuck wore cowboy boots and a John Deere cap and usually hung out with the three or four other wannabe cowboys at Highmont.

"Hey, guys," I said. I nodded to Tuck. "Tuck."

"Hey, Elroy." He held out his fist and I tapped it with mine. "Fire up."

"Fire up for what?" I asked.

"For getting out of class?"

"That'll work."

The assembly was for all the winter sports coming up: basketball, gymnastics, and wrestling. Basketball was out for me, I figured. I checked out the team. Looked like only one guy was under six feet tall. No, wait, he was the water boy. I moved on to gymnastics. They weren't all that big, plus they worked out in close proximity to the girls' team. This had possibilities. I watched them go through their demonstration.

Somehow Vern knew what I was thinking. He said, "So— the guy who can't touch his toes is considering gymnastics?"

"They're not very big. Look at them."

"Look what they're doing. It's about a million times more difficult than football."

"I'd have to concur," Tuck added.

They had a point. Football is mostly grunting and bumping into people and wearing armor while doing it. What could be more difficult than gymnastics? And so I turned my attention to the wrestling team. Wrestling had to be something I could learn. Competing only with guys my own size sounded good.

When the gymnasts finished their demonstration, the wrestlers dragged the mat to the center of the gym floor. I leaned forward. It was my last chance, the only sport left, unless I wanted to wait until April and go out for track. I couldn't wait that long for romance, I decided. Wrestling had to be it.

I watched closely. Todd Waylan and some other kid were going at it on the mat, tossing each other around. The match went back and forth, while the coach stood at the microphone calling out the moves as they were performed and the corresponding points.

"Fireman's carry—two points, Waylan. Two points, near fall. One-point escape, Thomas. Single leg, two points." And on and on.

You could tell it was staged. Kind of like the stuff you see on TV. They were going for all the spectacular stuff, which probably wouldn't work if they were wrestling live. But it was working. I was hooked. I liked the action.

I nudged Vern and pointed to the mat. "I could do this."

"Look at them, Elroy."

"I am."

"Look at them closely."

I was pretty sure I was seeing everything that was going on. "What do you mean?"

"They're wearing tights. They look like leprechauns."

First of all, leprechauns wore little shoes with curled-up toes. These guys definitely had regular feet. Besides, once I got pecs, I might look hot in a skintight wrestling uniform. "I could do this," I said again.

"Okay, don't say I didn't warn you. But I reserve the right to laugh at you."

I gave him a look.

"I mean in a nice way. If you dress up like a leprechaun, that is."

"Look at their shoes!" I yelled.

After the match, the coach invited everyone to try out for the wrestling team. He even emphasized the point that size didn't matter: You'd work out with guys your own weight. This sounded good to me. The members of the Second Base Club were proof that you had to be a jock to get anywhere with the opposite sex.

If it worked for them, it could work for me.

CHAPTER TEN

I finally did it. I made it to double digits on my pull-up tree. Then I added as many push-ups as I could, which wasn't many. Pull-ups usually wiped me out. Mom came home in the middle of my sit-up session.

I stood up and lifted my shirt. "Do I have abs yet?"

She squinted. "Hold on—I think I'm getting something." She pulled a magnifying glass from the junk drawer. "Come closer, let's have a look."

I pushed my shirt back down. "Never mind."

"I'm kidding," she said. "You're looking fit. What's going on? Working out for the bowling team?"

Mom was sly. She figured she'd avoid the direct tell-me-about-the-girl approach, hoping that I'd get around to it if she made like she wasn't interested. Little did she know that I didn't have anything to say. I had no stories to tell, let alone hide. Whatever I thought I had with Marisa was over.

"No bowling team, Mom. I think I might try wrestling."

"Wrestling?" She put on her concerned face. "Remember, Elroy, Highmont's school colors are green and more green."

"So?"

"Green tights, dear. I'm not sure how I feel about having a leprechaun in the family."

I let her make fun of the uniform. I didn't care. Wrestling was a means to an end. If dressing like an elf got me to second base or beyond, then it was worth it, even if my own mom teased me.

It took her a while to realize I was serious. But she finally understood. Maybe she didn't know my motivation, but she knew I meant business as far as the sport went. We drove to the Big 5 on Thompson, and I picked out a pair of wrestling shoes. "See?" I told her. "The toes aren't curled."

Once I had the shoes, or once she noticed that her purse was lighter by about forty dollars, she stopped cracking leprechaun jokes. I walked out of the store wearing the shoes. I felt like a jock, which filled me with hope in the girl department.

The next day, I met up with Vern at the usual spot and showed him the shoes. Vern just shook his head. "Marisa really must have gotten to you."

She had gotten to me, but that was beside the point. I had moved on. I'd put her behind me. At least, that's what I kept telling myself. How do you get over someone? What's the process? Maybe you just try and hope for the best.

After school, I showed up at the wrestling room. I wasn't sure what kind of clothes the team worked out in. I knew they wore tights for the matches, but I didn't know about the practices. I showed up in shorts and a T-shirt—and my new shoes.

Coach Grogan greeted me at the door. Well, he didn't exactly greet me. More like he sized me up, and it looked like he was holding back a laugh. Hey, maybe I didn't have pecs yet, but I was already into double digits on pull-ups. That had to count for something.

"Coach Grogan," he said finally, and held out his hand. I gave him mine and watched it get swallowed in his. He squeezed a little harder than necessary. Okay, a lot harder than necessary. He looked like a wrestler, stocky with mangled ears. He had Popeye forearms and a neck to match. Well, he really didn't have a neck. It was just a head connected to shoulders.

"Elroy."

"You ever wrestle before, Elroy?"

"Never," I told him. "But I've watched it on TV a lot."

He threw his head back and laughed. Then he plopped his huge hand on my shoulder and fixed me with a glare that would melt glass. "Son, that's not wrestling. It's bodybuilders who think they can act." He glanced at the mat, where there were four matches going on simultaneously. "Mike, come over here. The rest of you, clear off."

The wrestlers did as told, and one of them walked over. He looked smaller than me, and I was pretty sure he didn't have pecs. Of course, the sweatshirt he had on was baggy, but he didn't look like a guy I had to worry about.

Coach Grogan said, "Why don't you two wrestle for a few minutes. Start standing. If someone gets pinned, we'll start again. I want to see where we're at with Elroy here, skill-and-stamina–wise."

Pinned? That sounded good to me. There was nothing I'd like better than to pin one of the Highmont wrestlers in front of everybody. We went out to the center of the mat, and Mike held out his hand to me.

"It's nothing personal," he said.

And right then my confidence plummeted. I spun around and looked at the members of the team who were lining the mat. I saw the smirks. A few of them were shaking their heads. I looked back at Mike.

"Seriously, it's nothing personal," he said again.

Coach Grogan came between us and raised his hand, then brought it down like a karate chop. "Ready? Wrestle."

I figured I'd begin by grabbing a part of Mike. I'd watched the stuff a million times on TV. That's how it worked. I took a step forward . . . and suddenly I was in the air. Like some kind of involuntary cartwheel. My back hit the mat, followed by the rest of me. A second later, Coach Grogan slapped the mat and told us to start again.

Mike let go of me and helped me back to my feet.

"Ready? Wrestle."

This time it was different. There was no cartwheel, but I was in the air again. Then I was on my back again, and Mike was helping me up. I'd heard that lightning could strike twice in the same place, but I hadn't ever seen it. The question was, would it strike a third time? Not if I could help it.

Coach started us off again, and Mike came at me. I held up a hand and pointed to the door behind him. "Mike, is that your girlfriend? She's hot!" When he turned to check, I tackled him around the knees. He fell, and I landed on top of him.

Now what? Should I grab a knee? An elbow?

Mike didn't give me a chance to think about it. Before I knew it, he was on top of me. Then he whispered in my ear. No, it was more like a growl. "I said it was nothing personal. Now it is."

He bent me in a million different directions. Everything

was a tangle of body parts. I couldn't figure out where his left off and mine began. Or what to do. In desperation, I grabbed a foot and twisted. Pain shot through my ankle. Oops. Wrong foot.

Finally, Coach put a stop to the Elroy torture. I stood up, and the world was spinning. I'd just been beaten up by a guy smaller than me. Thank God no girls were around to see it.

"So how did it go?" Mom asked that evening. She saw that my face looked a little scuffed. "Scuffed" and "face" should never be used in the same sentence.

I really didn't want to talk about it, but Mom kept giving me the look.

"School was fine," I told her.

"I'm glad school went well." She leaned forward across the table, where we were seated. "How was wrestling practice?"

"Oh, that."

"It wasn't a pleasant experience. Is that what you're saying?" We were eating some kind of salad with chicken thrown on top. I longed for pancakes.

"I got beat up by a skinny kid." I reached up and touched the mat burn on the side of my face. "A little more brutal than I was expecting. I guess they wanted to see what I was made of."

"And did you show them?"

"I didn't cry."

After dinner, I did my homework and messed around with the guitar. I was getting pretty good with "Stairway to Heaven." When I couldn't keep my eyes open any longer, I made the couch into a bed and went to sleep.

The next morning, I couldn't move. My body ached all over. I hurt in places I'd never felt pain in before. I stared at the ceiling. Maybe if I started slow. I moved a toe, then a leg. . . . So far so good. I tried to sit up. Nope. Not working. I rolled out of bed and hit the floor with a thump.

Mom came running. She stood there looking at me with her hands on her hips.

"I don't suppose I could stay home from school?" I gave her my I'm-in-pain look. I wasn't acting.

"It'll pass," she said. She bent down and kissed me. "Gotta run. Get up and start moving; it's the best thing for workout pain."

I groaned and pushed myself up to a sitting position. A half-hour later, I was riding down Casitas Pass to meet Vern.

"I don't want you to take this the wrong way," Vern said when he saw me, "but there's something you gotta know."

"I'm all ears."

"You look like crap!"

"Thanks, friend."

"No problem." He smiled and told me to stay with it. "I'm thinking of joining the school newspaper. I'll come to your matches and write about them."

"No one writes about wrestling," I said.

"Exactly. You guys are unsung. The world has to know. Plus, you know what?"

"What?"

"Most of the *Highmont Herald* staff are girls. Chicks love the intellectual types."

I didn't know about that. Sampson Teague wasn't exactly known for his brain. "I'm going the jock route," I said. "We'll compare notes."

That afternoon, I continued my quest to become a jock.

When I walked into the wrestling room, Coach Grogan looked surprised. He came over. "You're back. Good. That says a lot. Mike was pretty rough with you yesterday. Sorry. I wanted to test your heart."

"Did I pass?"

"You did. Welcome to Highmont wrestling."

I was on a team for the first time in my life. I was also in pain, but it felt good for some reason.

CHAPTER ELEVEN

Turned out Mike was on varsity and was the best guy on the team after Todd Waylan. But that didn't matter, because there were three or four JV guys who could still kick my ass. And they did. Daily. I had mat burns on top of mat burns. I got so good at doing involuntary cartwheels that I think I could have done a voluntary one if asked.

I debated whether it was worth it. After one extremely bad beat-up-Elroy day, I went home and Googled all the monasteries in California. Might as well keep my options open. Maybe I was no more cut out for romance than I was for wrestling. But then I'd flash on those few moments I'd had with Marisa and think, yes, I'd keep at this. It *was* worth it.

Mom had tons of workout advice for me, mostly about how to cope with soreness. She worked at a spa; it was her area of expertise. "The first few weeks are the toughest," she told me. "If you stay with it, your body will adjust."

That was a little hard to believe, but by the end of the second week of practice, I found that she was right. I could walk without pain. I could get out of bed like a normal person. And then something else happened. Something amazing and, well, shocking.

I was in the bathroom one morning brushing my teeth when I saw it. "Mom! Come quick!" I screamed.

She came running. "What is it?"

"Look." I pointed to my bare chest. "Pecs!"

"Where? Let me get the magnifying glass." But she was smiling. "Looking good, Elroy. And you're no longer sore, right?"

"Right."

I still had the mental humiliation of getting my ass kicked on a daily basis, but at least I felt good physically. And I looked better. Now, if only I could get someone to notice. I began wearing tighter shirts and putting my pecs out there for the world to see, especially during fourth-period math. Someone had to notice. They had to!

I wasn't the only one looking good. After practice on Friday, I rode over to my dad's studio apartment. I wouldn't have to start worrying about making weight for a while. Bring on those carbs—I was looking forward to a weekend of pancakes.

I carried my bike up the stairs to the apartment door and knocked. No answer. The lights were out. "Dad? You there? It's Elroy."

I was about to get out my cell phone and dial Mom when Dad showed up. Actually, he jogged up. He was in shorts and had on running shoes, an iPod strapped to his arm. He pulled out the ear buds. "Hey, Elroy. Want to compare abs?"

"I'd win," I told him.

"Probably, but I'd give you a run for your money."

He looked good. In fact, he looked great. The best I'd seen him in a long time. And it wasn't only physical. It was the way he carried himself. Confidence? I don't know, maybe he was just . . . happy. "Looking good, Dad."

"It's all part of the plan," he said.

We went inside, and Dad started mixing up the pancake batter for dinner.

"What plan is that?" I asked.

"Changes, Elroy. Just making some changes. How's your mother?"

"She's doing okay. How are things in the wild kingdom?"

"Another day, another pit bull. I have a few other irons in the fire, though. At least mentally."

I looked over at his whiteboard. It was still just an empty rectangle.

Dad saw me looking and said, "Not all of my thoughts are visible to the human eye, Elroy."

I nodded. "I guess that's a good sign. I'd be worried if the contents of your brain could be contained on this board."

"Me too."

Still, a blank whiteboard didn't give me much to go on.

Dad finished mixing the batter and walked over. "Just to set the record straight, working for Animal Control is not permanent. I have a new venture in the works."

Even with his off-kilter nose, he was a good-looking guy. And now, as he talked about his future, his eyes were ablaze with hope. It was hard not to believe in him. The only thing that made me doubt was his track record. He'd failed three times in the restaurant business, and here he was, talking about throwing his hat in the ring again. Maybe not the restaurant ring, but some ring. Some soon-to-be-named ring.

I looked at the empty rectangle, trying hard to read between the horizontal lines. "Dad, Mom's not too keen on your business ventures."

"I know that, Elroy. This time will be different. I won't go forward unless it comes together. I'll know when it's right."

"So what's the idea?"

"You are on an as-need-to-know basis," he said.

"I need to know, Dad. I really do. Your future and mine are kind of linked, you know?"

He nodded. "I'll fill you in soon. I promise." He headed to the bathroom. "Now, go make us some pancakes. I'm going to get cleaned up."

I cooked while Dad took a shower. After dinner, we got out the Scrabble. He took the first game, but I paid him back on the second. Triple word score for OXEN. And in between, he filled me in on how to catch a raccoon, while I filled him in on my latest— actually my first—foray into sports, high-school or otherwise.

"Okay, let's not compare abs," he said.

We did anyway. He lost.

The next night, I worked at Ernesto's along with Juana Maria.

"Hi, Elroy. How's it going?"

"Great," I told her.

She had on her off-the-shoulder blouse, along with her peasant-girl skirt, and a yellow flower in her hair. It was another busy night. Juana Maria helped out making salads here and there, but mostly she helped me (or I helped her) seat customers.

Things started to slow sometime after nine, and we stood together near the entrance and wrapped silverware in cloth napkins. It felt good not to be in a rush for a change. And having someone to talk to wasn't too shabby either.

"So what kind of music do you like?" she asked. She pulled the fake flower from her hair and tossed it on the lectern.

"I like anything musical."

"How about narrowing that down a bit?"

"Current stuff. Old stuff."

She tapped me on the head with a spoon. "Thank you, Mr. Vague. Details, man."

"Rock and roll, mostly. Some pop and R & B. I just have one criterion when it comes to music." I plopped a rolled napkin on the stack and reached for the silverware.

"And that is?"

"It has to sound good."

"You're smarter than you look, Elroy."

"Thanks," I said. "What about you? What kind of music do you like?"

"I like country music."

I shot her a look. "Country? You mean like Shania Twang?"

"It's not all twang."

Maybe not, but I sure wouldn't listen to it. "Would it be okay if I made fun of you for the rest of the night?" I asked her.

"Why would you want to do that?"

"You like country. Need I say more?"

She made a fist and held it up. "And you're begging for a charley horse."

After the last customer left, Ernesto poked his head out of his office and told us we could take off anytime.

"Walk a girl to her car?"

"Sure."

I grabbed my sweatshirt and pulled it on as we went outside. It was colder than I was expecting—we could see our breath—but I knew I'd warm up on the ride home.

She turned and faced me once we reached her car. "You know something, Elroy?"

"What?"

"You have the strangest-looking acne I've ever seen."

"They're mat burns," I said. "I'm on the Highmont wrestling team."

"Really?"

"Yeah, why?"

"You look more like the bowling-team type."

Why did people keep saying that? I had the sudden urge to rip off my shirt and show her I had more than a bowling-team body. "You haven't seen my pecs."

"Please. I just ate."

I stood there a moment, trying to come up with a good comeback. Finally, I grabbed her car keys, chirped the alarm, and opened her door. "Get home safe," I told her.

"A gentleman," she said as she got in. "You just scored points."

"That was the plan." It wasn't really. But I liked being called a gentleman by a cute girl—a very cute girl. A very cute girl with a psycho for a father, but still. . . .

"Really?" She looked up at me, smiling. A guy could get used to a smile like that. It was a darn shame about her father. "What plan is that?"

"I'm not sure yet."

"No plan?"

I pointed to my chest. "Completely planless here."

"Jeez, Elroy. I think I'm insulted." She laughed. Then she drove off, leaving a hint of her perfume behind.

I was still sitting on the other side of the room from Marisa in math. I willed myself not to look her way, but I couldn't help myself. Every molecule in my body ached with what-could-have-been and what-almost-was. I had no idea how to move past it. Focus on something else, I figured.

I now sat across the aisle from Carol Ann. She wasn't exactly a Marisa Caldwell, but she was not bad-looking at all. I thought of various break-the-ice lines: *Isn't this the best triceps you've seen in a while? Wanna see my abs? In case you're wondering, this isn't acne.* But they all seemed lame.

Once again, I decided to be direct. No-frills flirting. Say something and see where it leads.

I faced her. "How was your weekend, Carol Ann?"

She turned and looked at me, then glanced to either side of her, as if there could be two people in the room with that name. She wore her hair short and didn't overdo the makeup. A clean look and, like I said, not bad.

"It was good," she said finally. Then, after a pause, she added with a smile, "Thanks."

It was a start, I figured.

I met up with Vern at lunch. He was sitting with Tuck Mayfield at our usual spot in the quad. Tuck held out a fist, and I smacked it with mine.

"Fire up."

"So, Tuck, what's the deal? First you sit with us at the assembly, and now you hang with us at lunch. Aren't you usually with the other cowboys?"

"Taking a break," Tuck said. He crossed his booted legs and

yanked off his John Deere hat. "Also, I'm trying to kick the chewing-tobacco habit. Need to watch who I hang out with."

"Good idea," I said.

"Yeah, but I really miss the spitting."

"I don't blame you."

CHAPTER TWELVE

I was on my back. Some guy was on top of me, his armpit covering my face. He must have been boycotting deodorant, and I was pretty sure he hadn't showered in the last year. If I inhaled, I was a goner. If I didn't breathe, I wouldn't survive. What to do?

Somehow I got to my stomach and began to crawl for the door. He was on top of me trying to pull me back, but I was on a mission. I needed air, and maybe I just had to admit to myself that wrestling wasn't for me.

"Where are you going, Elroy?" Coach Grogan yelled.

I reached the door and stood up. Then I looked at Coach and at Smelly Armpits, both of them staring at me like I'd lost my mind. Nah . . . I'd finally come to my senses. I could find a better use for my time. I liked having pecs and abs, but I'd have to find a way to keep them without sniffing armpits.

"Sorry, Coach," I said, and to Smelly Armpits I added, "It's nothing personal." I headed for the locker room.

✦ ✦ ✦

"You quit?" Vern asked the next day.

"I didn't say I quit." But I was thinking about it. Seriously.

"Well, you played hooky right in the middle of practice." Vern thought for a second. "Is there such a thing as AWOL in high-school sports?"

I didn't know, and, frankly, I didn't care how you labeled it. I was just tired of getting my ass kicked for the sake of something that might never happen. The only thing that stopped me was the Second Base Club. Obviously, the sports angle worked for them.

"What are your parents going to say?" Vern asked.

That was a good question. I think my sporty mom liked the idea that I'd finally found a sport, that I was part of a team and working out. She wouldn't make quitting easy.

"I was going to write about you for the *Herald*." He made quotation marks. " 'Elroy Gets Thumped.' "

"Yeah, I don't want to miss that."

"Neither do I. Your fifteen minutes of fame—and mine."

I kicked around the idea of quitting for the next couple of days. Meanwhile, I went back to practice. Coach didn't look happy.

"What was that about yesterday?" he asked me.

"I'm not sure," I told him.

"I'll give you one of those, Elroy. Just one. If it happens again, don't bother coming back."

That was fair enough. You couldn't very well run a team if there was no consequence for going AWOL. Still, I didn't know what to do. How could I quit and hold my head up? More important, how could I get anywhere in the girl department without going out for a sport? Wasn't that the whole basis for the Second Base Club? They were all jocks, united with one purpose. I racked my brain, trying to come up with an answer.

And then it came to me.

I met up with Vern and Tuck in the quad at lunch. "I'll wrestle one match," I said.

Vern and Tuck exchanged a look. "What?"

"I'll wrestle one JV match. Then I'll quit. You can still write your article, Vern." I made quotation marks. " 'Elroy Thumps.' "

Vern and Tuck nodded.

"I can live with that," Vern said.

"I'll be there too," Tuck added. He pulled a can of Skoal out of his back pocket.

"I thought you were giving that up," I said.

"I am." He opened the can and held it out for me to see. It was filled with little candies. "Mint?"

Vern and I grabbed some.

"If this was filled with tobacco, I'd be thrown out of school. Contraband, you know? And you know what else? Girls don't like kissing a guy who chews tobacco. It's—"

"Like licking an ashtray?" I asked.

"Worse."

And so that was my plan. I'd stay with wrestling until my first match, one I hoped to win, then I'd move on. Continue with the *real* quest.

Along that line, I had three more chats with Carol Ann in math. I also struck up conversations with Cynthia in biology and Tess in history. Putting all of your eggs in one basket was always a bad idea.

Meanwhile, I kept an eye on the Second Base Club. Maybe I could pick up a pointer or two, or just absorb some of their confidence and swagger. Actually, I'd been practicing my swagger when I thought no one was looking. After a while I gave it up. It was exhausting. I was self-conscious enough as it was. I didn't need to be thinking about how I was walking all the time. Besides, Juana Maria once asked me why I was limping. Clearly, my swagger was sending out the wrong message.

Chapter Thirteen

"**W**hat is it?" I asked. I was in Vern's garage, and I wasn't sure what I was looking at.

But Vern certainly was excited. "What do you mean, what is it? See the steering wheel? See the tires?"

I saw two wheels. And the glass was too dirty for me to see inside.

"Come on, Vern. I need a hint."

He gave me a look. "Don't you know a babe mobile when you see one? Or are you in love with the idea of riding your bike for the rest of your life?"

He had a point. I took a second look at the vehicle in front of me. Only two wheels—okay, that was fixable. Missing a couple of fenders—again, fixable. I circled the car, looking it over. It was a Volkswagen Bug from the early sixties. A very faint blue. Vern had turned sixteen on October 7 and got his license the same day. Now he had a car. A major clunker, but still.

"Does it have an engine?" I went around to the front and grabbed the hood.

"Engine's in the back," Vern said.

I knew that. I was just testing him. I kept circling, running my hand over the numerous dents. It was a car. It was definitely a car, and I was beginning to see the possibilities. The girl possibilities. The makeout possibilities.

I stopped and looked up at Vern. "Does it run?"

"Not yet. Needs a new battery, fuel pump, spark plugs, and of course gas." According to Vern, it hadn't run for at least ten years; it just sat there under a tarp.

We went around the back and took a look at the engine. "Rats!" Vern yelled. The engine compartment was filled with scraps of paper, twigs, and rat poop.

But there was an engine inside. Even though it had been lived in by rodents, I saw the potential. I was actually kind of envious. Vern had his own car. A nonrunning, rat-infested one—still, it was more than I had.

"Tell you what," I told him. "You clean out the rat leftovers. I'll help you with everything else."

I was really getting tired of riding my bike everywhere. If we could get this thing running, I was all for it.

"Deal," he said. He put on gardening gloves and got busy with the dirty work.

Meanwhile, I grabbed a rubber mallet and began pounding out some of the more obvious dents. Was I making more dents than I was fixing? Probably. But I loved swinging that mallet. It felt creative and destructive at the same time.

Three weeks later, we were driving down Thompson, the main drag of Highmont. The car was still missing two fenders, had a cracked windshield, and was way too loud, but it sure beat traveling by bike.

Vern had to pump the brakes to bring the car to a stop. We also found that there were no seat belts.

"I dub thee the Death Trap," I said.

Vern agreed that this was the perfect name. We called it the Trap for short.

"What is it?" This time it was Tuck circling the car and scratching his head.

Vern rolled his eyes. I don't think he appreciated that Tuck and I had a similar sense of humor.

It was the day before Thanksgiving, and since I had my one and only wrestling match coming up, I wouldn't be partaking in most of the eating. I'd have a stalk of celery and call it a day. I still had to shed a few pounds to make weight.

Tuck kept circling the Volkswagen. "Wait, wait. It's coming to me. It's a car, right?" He laughed, pulled out the Skoal tin from his back pocket, and offered Vern a mint. I took one too. "I'm only kidding, Vern. It's great. How does it feel to have a car?"

"Pretty fantastic," he said, and Tuck and I shot him envious looks.

Just like me, Tuck saw the possibilities. He began opening the doors, checking the trunk and engine department. "We need to break this car in properly."

"Cruise night?" I suggested.

Tuck shook his head. "Something bigger than cruise night. We need a road trip."

Tuck was right. We needed more than cruising down Thompson on a Friday night. We had to go somewhere far away. Spend a night or two. It was Vern's first car, and we needed to celebrate it. "What do you say, Vern?" Tuck asked.

"Sounds like a plan. Where do you have in mind?"

"Templin Highway. We can be there in two hours. You guys got sleeping bags?"

Vern and I nodded.

"And I'll bring the Coleman stove," I said.

"I'll bring the tent," Tuck said. "Vern, you want to bring the food?"

"I'm the guy with the vehicle."

"Good point. Okay, Elroy and I will get the food. Fire up." Tuck held out his fist, and Vern and I smacked it.

The plan was to leave the morning after our various Thanksgiving celebrations. As I said, mine would be fairly minimal—a stalk of celery; maybe I'd allow myself a salad with oil-and-vinegar dressing. Of course, part of the fun of camping is all the great food you get to eat while trying to survive in the outdoors. I never should have joined the wrestling team.

My grandparents from my mom's side lived above the junior college. Yes, in you-know-who's neighborhood. I willed myself not to think that Marisa was only a few blocks away, but it didn't work. When we passed her street, I couldn't help looking, trying to get a glimpse, and my stomachache came back just to let me know it had been there all along, waiting for this opportunity.

My grandfather wasn't wealthy or anything, just a guy who bought a house on the hill ages ago, when it was still affordable for the average person. That wasn't the case anymore.

We arrived at the house around two o'clock and stayed until six. I stuck with the noneating plan. Maybe, if I ate nothing for

Thanksgiving dinner, I could allow myself something during the Celebrate Vern's New (Old) Car Camping Extravaganza. That was my plan, anyway.

My grandpa thought I was on drugs. "A young man like you, not eating?" He made me stand on one foot and count to thirty. Then he had me close my eyes, hold my arms out to the sides, and touch my nose.

"Want me to walk a straight line?" I asked after passing both tests. "You watch too many cop shows, Grandpa."

"I miss *Magnum, P.I.* Private eyes these days are wimps. A man needs facial hair."

Mom came to my rescue. "Dad, Elroy isn't eating because he's on the wrestling team and has to make weight on Tuesday."

"Grow some facial hair, Elroy," Grandpa grumbled. "It will intimidate your opponents."

"I'll give it some thought." Actually, facial hair is against the rules in high-school wrestling, but I didn't tell him that.

I could hear the Death Trap from a mile away as it struggled up Casitas Pass. Mom came running from her bedroom.

"What's that noise?" She peered out the window at the dark clouds moving in. Looked like a storm. But this was not the rumble she was hearing.

"The Death Trap," I told her. "Vern's car."

"His car is called the Death Trap?" She had on her worried look, which was almost as bad as her scan-the-back-of-my-skull look. "Am I supposed to feel good about this?"

"It's just a name, Mom," I said, opening the door as Vern and Tuck pulled up. I grabbed my gear and went outside to meet them.

Mom followed me. She walked up to the car and gave it a

long look, then glanced at Vern. "I'm trying to be open-minded, Vern. I really am."

Vern looked at me and rolled his eyes. I think he was getting tired of people making cracks about his car, or hinting that it wasn't road-worthy.

"It's not as bad as it looks," Vern told her.

"Yeah, but it looks *really* bad," Mom said. "I mean, *really.*"

The back seat of the car was piled with camping gear. A few fishing rods dangled out the passenger-side window. I barely found room to squeeze in.

Mom still looked worried. "Death Trap is just a name," I yelled over the sound of the engine. "We'll be back on Sunday." Then I whispered to Vern, "Let's go before she changes her mind."

Vern nodded and put the car in gear, and we took off down Casitas Pass.

"Where are we going again?" I asked.

"Templin Highway. Fire up."

I *was* fired up. I wanted to get away, shake out a few cobwebs.

Tuck said, "How about some music?"

"I'm working on getting a good stereo. For now, all we have is an AM radio, which only picks up the more powerful stations from L.A."

"You mean—"

"Yes, not much to listen to unless you're a big Rush Limbaugh fan."

"What's a road trip with no music?" I started in on "99 Bottles of Beer," and Tuck and Vern joined in, but we only made it to ninety-two before stopping. Too much math involved; it seemed like homework. We headed away from the coast on the 126, passing through Santa Paula and Fillmore. Then we turned north on the I-5, and it began to rain.

"Shit!"

"What's wrong?"

Vern rolled down his window and stuck his head out as the storm kicked into high gear. "Windshield wipers aren't working. Tuck, roll down your window. Tell me if I'm going to hit anything on that side."

For some reason, none of us thought of turning back. We pressed on toward Templin Highway, Vern and Tuck with their heads out the window, then turned off the interstate after about an hour and followed a tiny road that wound its way through the Los Padres National Forest. This was no forest at all. Mostly yucca and mustard plants, with a few oaks and willows along the creek.

"This is it," Tuck said. "Turn here."

It was a tiny dirt (now mud) road that led down to the creek. Vern turned onto it and followed it to the water's edge.

"We better get the tent up."

We got out of the car, and the rain came at us sideways, which made it almost impossible to get the tent up. What made it *completely* impossible was that we had no tent poles. We had a tent, but we had no way to set it up. And while we stood there thinking about it, the storm grew worse. Tuck held on to his cowboy hat so it wouldn't blow away. "Sorry, guys," he yelled over the sound of the wind and rain.

"Now what?" I yelled back.

Tuck looked at Vern, who looked at his car parked in the mud. "Let's get out of the rain."

And that's how a 1961 Volkswagen Beetle became our motor home for the weekend. It rained all night. We couldn't cook with propane in such confined quarters. Instead, we ended up eating cold chili out of the can, which later came back to haunt us, if you know what I mean.

"Roll down a window, Vern," I said. "I can't breathe."

"It's raining."

"I'd rather get wet than suffocate."

I think that was the consensus—we needed air. We could deal with the water, but not the lack of oxygen. Vern and Tuck rolled down the windows.

"Anyone who farts more than their share sleeps outside," Tuck said. "I mean it."

Was he serious? A gas quota? I'd never heard of such a thing. I squeezed my cheeks together until I realized that I was the only one holding back. Tuck kept asking me and Vern to pull his finger. I wouldn't do it—I absolutely refused.

What a way to celebrate Vern's new set of wheels. We sat up all night in our sleeping bags, sleepless, wet, and farting.

CHAPTER FOURTEEN

Okay, so I starved myself on Thanksgiving and ate a fair amount of chili at Templin Highway and the Night of Gas. I wasn't sure if you could lose weight by farting, but somehow I felt lighter. On Monday, I headed to the wrestling room before school to weigh myself. I was three pounds over weight. No problem. I could lose that during practice.

After school, I went to the locker room to change. Football season was over, but I noticed several members of the Second Base Club lingering. They were like kids without a clubhouse. They needed a place to meet, and the locker room seemed the logical location, since the one thing they had in common (besides their point system) was that they were all jocks.

One guy had his locker open, and the others were gathered around him. I laced up my wrestling shoes—slowly, on purpose. I had my reasons. First, I wanted to delay the ass-whupping I'd receive in the wrestling room, but mostly I wanted the latest news from the Second Base Club. These guys were obviously doing something right. Maybe I could pick up a few pointers.

The guy with the open locker said, "Sampson's in double digits, gentlemen."

A few club members hooted and slapped high-fives. Some others cursed.

"Who's in second?"

"Jerry's in second with nine."

That would be Jerry the tight end on the football team. He was there, looking over the shoulder of the guy reading the list.

"Evan and Sam are tied for third. It's early. It's still anyone's game." He closed his locker and looked down the aisle toward me. Our eyes locked.

"You want something, homo?" he said.

I knew a rhetorical question when I heard one. I grabbed my other shoe out of my locker and headed for the wrestling room. But I couldn't stop thinking about Sampson Teague. Double digits? Did that mean he'd hit a couple of home runs? Or had he just gotten to first base ten times? And how many of those points were scored with my former almost-girlfriend?

When I got to the wrestling room, Coach Grogan was there writing on the blackboard. In one column he'd listed the thirteen weight classes, from ninety-eight pounds to heavyweight. Beside this were the names of the wrestlers and what division they'd be competing in—JV or varsity.

Coach looked at me. "Elroy," he said in a voice that seemed way too cheerful for my no-neck wrestling coach, "do I have news for you."

A few things raced through my mind. *I'm kicked off the team? We need a water boy, and would I mind not wrestling—ever?*

"Guess who's wrestling varsity tomorrow?"

I glanced at the 123-pound spot on the board, where only one name was listed. Mine.

"What?!"

"Mike is dropping down to 115 for the season. The others are out with injuries or illnesses. Which leaves you in the varsity spot at 123."

"What?" I said again.

I'd seen what a varsity wrestler could do to a guy like me. I'd endured three lifetimes' worth of involuntary cartwheels.

"Coach, you've seen me wrestle. I can't even beat the JV guys."

He continued writing on the board. "If we forfeit, we give the other team six points. If you get pinned, they get six points. The way I see it, all you have to do is avoid getting pinned and you'll be helping the team. Stay off your back, Elroy. That's all I'm asking."

Thanks for the vote of confidence. My plan to end the season with a perfect 1–0 record seemed impossible. Butterflies churned inside me. The match was still a day away, but my knees were already knocking.

"All right, warm up," Coach yelled. "Elroy, work with Mike." Then, under his breath, "You're going to need it."

I prayed for an injury. I didn't resist as Mike tossed me on my head half a dozen times. But by the end of practice, I was still intact. Three pounds lighter, but still intact.

On Tuesday, during lunch, we hauled the mat to the gym and set up some chairs for the teams to sit on. Vern was there with a pad of yellow paper. He pulled a pencil from behind his ear.

"So, Elroy, how does it feel to be wrestling varsity? Are you nervous? Scared?"

Me, nervous? Just because some Neanderthal was going to pull my arms from their sockets? Just because there was going to be an audience witnessing the event? I wasn't nervous at all. I was terrified!

But I tried not to show it. "Why do you want to know?" I asked

"I told you, I joined the *Highmont Herald*."

"Have you written anything yet?"

"No, but I think I've found my calling."

"Any cute girls on the newspaper staff?"

"Tons." He tapped his pencil on the yellow pad. "Now, back to my question. Your thoughts on your match tonight."

I wasn't about to tell him what I really thought. That taking an ass-whupping by your own teammate was one thing, but a real match was different. Mostly because it would be a public event. People would come to watch this thing. Perfect strangers would see some guy twist me into a pretzel.

"Just come to the match and write about what happens," I told him. But I think my face said it all—I *was* nervous; I *was* scared. The butterflies in my stomach morphed into something bat-sized.

"I'll be there," Vern said. "Just poking around for more material to flesh out the story."

First of all, I wasn't the story. The whole team was the story. And second, if I was going to take a public ass-kicking, I wasn't sure I wanted someone chronicling the event.

For the rest of the school day, I imagined my opponent. I even doodled what he might look like and gave him a title—Igor the One-Eye. I pictured some kid with big muscles who drooled a lot and whose hands hung below his knees. I was pretty sure that was who they'd match me up with, a drooling Igor the One-Eye.

I couldn't focus in class. My short life kept flashing before my eyes. I was going to die, all in the name of school athletics, and Vern was going to make a record of it. Well, at least my parents would have something to remember me by.

After school, the other team showed up in a beat-up bus that had to be fifty years old.

They were from Saint Aquinas, the local Catholic school, which was not known for much—except wrestling. They got off the bus, and I looked for my one-eyed opponent. Everyone had two eyes. I scanned for drool. Not a spot of dribble anywhere. But one of them had extra-long arms. Later, in the locker room, when they called out the 123-pound weight class for weigh-ins, this was the guy who stepped up.

So I wasn't going up against a Cyclops or a drooler. But those arms looked scary. I imagined them doing painful things to me, bending me in ways no human should be bent.

I went to my locker and got into my green singlet and tights. I didn't care that I looked like a leprechaun. This was my one and only match. Tomorrow, my season would be over. I could move on.

Coach pulled me aside before the match. "Remember what I said, Elroy. Stay off your back and you'll be helping the team."

"Got it, Coach." My stomach lurched at the thought of walking out onto the mat—alone. No backup. Just me and my knuckle-dragging opponent.

We went out to the gym, which was more crowded than I

expected. Family members, mostly. I saw my mom and dad sitting together near the top of the bleachers, and right then my butterflies doubled. As far as I knew, my parents didn't talk at all, and here they were, sitting together. Mom blew me a kiss. Dad gave me the thumbs-up. A few minutes later, Vern walked in with his yellow pad, followed by Tuck, who had on what looked like his Sunday best: boot jeans that were almost creased and a belt buckle so shiny it caught the reflection of the overhead fluorescent lighting.

Vern walked over and clicked his pen. "So, Elroy, any last words? I mean, any thoughts?"

"My parents are here," I said.

He looked up at the bleachers, located them, gave a nod. "That's good, right?"

"I need some air," I told him. I went outside, and he followed. Two girls walked by and gave a long stare at my green tights, smirking as they continued past.

"Wrestling team," Vern said in my defense. Then he turned to me. "What is it? Nerves?"

"My parents are here," I said again.

"You're their offspring. It happens. Did you think they'd skip your high-school sports debut?"

"I don't know."

"Parents showing up is a good thing."

"More pressure, I guess." But I knew that wasn't it. Mom and Dad sitting together was something I hadn't seen in more than a year. I went back to the doorway of the gym and looked inside. My parents were watching Aquinas go through their warmups. I couldn't read their expressions. Were they simply tolerating an uncomfortable situation for my sake? Or was something deeper going on?

My stomach made a noise, and Vern heard it. He gestured to my gut with his pen. "Can I quote that?"

I gave him a hard look.

"Seriously. I have no idea how to spell it, but what a great quote."

I gazed back to my parents, who were now staring my way and waving.

Vern shoved me from behind back into the gym. "Better get in there, Elroy. Your coach is looking a little peeved. My advice, concentrate on your match. Family worries can wait."

"Yeah. Good advice, Vern," I said as the butterflies hammered against my ribs.

"But before you go, got a quote for me?"

"Just watch and report what you see."

I headed back toward my team. Tuck jogged over and offered me a mint from his back-pocket Skoal can. I took two.

The more I thought about it, the more I liked that my parents were sitting together and seeming to get along. I had no idea what it meant, but I liked it. And that's where I left it. I turned my attention back to the mat.

After the JVs wrestled, they started the varsity match, beginning with the ninety-eight-pounders and moving up. Aquinas looked tough. Neither our ninety-eight- nor our hundred-and-six-pounder went the distance. But I knew Mike would be a different story. And he did not disappoint. It was nice to see someone else doing involuntary cartwheels for a change. But there was a downside—the match ended quickly.

Before I knew it, I was on. The butterflies churned in my stomach and started clambering up my throat. Any second, I was going to throw up. I was sure of it.

I glanced up at the stands, which were more crowded than

they'd been a few minutes before. Some guys I'd seen around school sat in the first row. *Crap.* They'd see my ass-whupping up close and personal.

Fake an injury, I told myself. It was my only way out.

"Let's go, Elroy," Coach yelled. "Keep it going."

Too late—showtime. My heart throbbed as I strapped on my headgear and went out to shake hands with Long-Arms. I could feel the blood draining from my face. And my opponent was smirking, like he knew that I was no varsity wrestler, that this was going to be quick and painless . . . at least for him.

I looked up at the stands one last time. Mom and Dad were staring right at me. Vern and Tuck were rooting me on. And that's when it hit me. Maybe I could do this. Maybe I could do more than stay off my back. I looked across the mat at my opponent, who was trying to stare me down. I returned the gaze.

"You won't get any cartwheels out of me without my consent," I mumbled under my breath.

The ref blew the whistle, and I went after Long-Arms.

The next day, Vern's article came out in the *Highmont Herald.* Turns out, the guy can write.

HIGHMONT WRESTLERS TAKE ON AQUINAS
by Vern Zuckman

Last night the Highmont Raiders wrestling team hosted the returning league champs, the Thomas Aquinas Saints. As expected it was business as usual for the Saints, with three notable exceptions—Mike Thomas, Todd Waylan, and first-year wrestler Elroy Tillman, who, at the request of Coach Bill Grogan, filled the varsity spot minutes before the match began.

"He pulled off a win against a tough wrestler from a very tough school," said Grogan. "I was impressed and a little shocked."

So were most of those in attendance.

From the opening whistle, Tillman took the offensive, scoring a takedown in the first few seconds of the match in what seemed to be some sort of forced cartwheel. The Aquinas wrestler soon escaped, and then, just to show that it wasn't a fluke, or possibly that lightning could indeed strike twice in the same place, Elroy Tillman did it again—he forced his opponent into another involuntary cartwheel. The Highmont wrestlers lining the mat were on their feet, cheering on their new teammate, who then turned it on, scoring near fall after near fall. Tillman won the match 15–10.

"He was amazing," said spectator Tuck Mayfield. "I'd hate to meet Elroy in a dark alley. . . ."

I don't know what got into me. Maybe knowing that it was my one and only match and that I had nothing to lose took the pressure off. I gave it my all because it was the only time I'd have to. In any case, it was nice of Vern to make me the focus of his debut article.

But the more I thought about it, the more I realized that it made no sense to quit. I'd kicked ass in a match. I'd made another human being do cartwheels at my bidding. And if I kept wrestling, my parents would have to sit together for the next three months. How could I take that lightly?

I couldn't. True, there were no girls my age at the match, so the romance angle—the original reason for joining the wrestling team—no longer applied. I wouldn't gain anything in the girl department by continuing to wrestle. But there were too many reasons to keep at it.

I'd have to find another way to get some girl's attention.

CHAPTER FIFTEEN

The girl quest continued. I went out to my oak tree before school and did eleven pull-ups. Then I added a few push-ups and sat on the front steps of the Airstream and waited for Vern. My best friend had a car. Life would never be the same.

Vern pulled up a few minutes later, and Mom came to the door, thinking a tornado was kicking up and I'd better get inside. If it was a tornado, I certainly didn't want to find refuge in a trailer. "It's okay, Mom. It's just Vern."

She stood there in her robe and slippers, looking out through the screen door. "Yes, I can see that," she said as Vern pulled up. "The Death Trap, right?"

"Yeah." The Death Trap now had four fenders. It was still way too loud, had a crappy sound system, and looked like it was going to fall apart any second. But at least it had all its parts.

I gave a wave. "See you later, Mom." I got in and we took off.

"So you know what tonight is?" Vern asked.

"What's tonight?"

"Friday night. Highmont Ridge cruise night."

I'd forgotten. Cruise night was something I'd never participated in. With no car, there was no reason to. Now we had the Death Trap.

"Let's ask Tuck to join us," I said.

Vern nodded. We needed someone with confidence along for the ride. Tuck wasn't an in-crowder, but he carried himself as if he was. If we spent enough time with him, maybe some of it would rub off.

We met up with Tuck in the quad at lunch. "Gentlemen," he said, "fire up for cruise night." Obviously, he'd been thinking the same thing. "Vern's car isn't pretty, but it will get the job done."

I wasn't sure what he meant, but I had an idea. "Job done" sounded like "second base" to me.

Vern picked me up that evening at seven. For once Mom didn't rush to the door, thinking a tornado was racing up the canyon. "Hi, Vern," she said, without looking up from her book. "Don't stay out too late, Elroy."

"I won't," I said and was out the door before she could give me a specific time. Late was a vague concept, and I wanted to keep it that way.

"Where's Tuck?" I asked Vern as I got in on the passenger side.

"Wanted to give you first dibs at riding shotgun."

"Good boy."

Tuck was out in his front yard casting his fly line when we pulled up. He reeled in the line and stowed it in the garage, then walked over. "Templin Highway was a bust, guys."

"No shit," I said.

"Although it smelled like it," Vern added, fanning the air.

Tuck got in behind me, and I shut the door. He said, "What I'm saying is, we haven't celebrated Vern's car properly yet."

"What did you have in mind?"

"The Eastern Sierra during spring break."

"I'm in," I said.

But spring break was three months away. For now we had cruise night to think about. Vern put the car in gear, and we headed out to Thompson.

The speed limit along Thompson was thirty-five miles per hour. Way too fast to see anything. And definitely too fast to flirt. Vern kept the speedometer at about fifteen miles per hour, which seemed to be the going pace, and we checked out the sights. The cars that weren't inching along were parked along the curb. Sidewalks were packed with Highmont's teenagers. Music blasted from car stereos. Some people (girls) were dancing, some had on Rollerblades—everyone hoping to be noticed.

I did a quick zit-check in the side mirror. Not a pimple in sight. And the scuff marks from wrestling were hardly visible. I'd been working on ways to get beat up during practice without getting scuffed.

Vern pulled up to a stoplight. Three girls stood on the corner and were looking our way.

I turned to Vern and Tuck. "What do I do?"

"Say something, stupid," Tuck said.

"Say something stupid? Wouldn't it be better to say something intelligent?"

"Say something, you idiot!"

The girls were still looking at us. "What do I say?"

The car behind us honked. Too late. The light was green, and Vern stepped on the gas.

"Pull over, Vern," Tuck said. "Elroy, let me out."

"You're leaving?"

"No, I'm sitting shotgun. Gonna show you bozos how it's done. Watch and learn."

Vern found an open spot at the curb and pulled over, but I wasn't about to give up my seat. "I can do this. You just have to be patient, Tuck." I turned to Vern. "Circle the block. See if those girls are still there."

But the girls were no longer there when we came by a second time.

Tuck said, "Just be friendly, Elroy. That's all. If you can't be witty or charming, just be friendly. Chicks dig that. You're thinking too much. You're trying way too hard."

Maybe he was right. I could do friendly. When we reached the end of town, Vern turned the car around and we made another pass.

"There." Tuck pointed. "Three girls." It was a different three. "Vern, stop at the light."

"What if it's green?"

"Stop anyway."

I glanced at the speedometer—thirteen miles per hour, then twelve, eleven. Vern kept slowing down. The car behind us honked.

"Yellow light! Good driving, Vern."

He stopped the car at the intersection, which put us right next to the three girls. Tuck slapped my shoulder. "Elroy, you're on."

"Just be friendly?" I whispered.

"Yes. Friendly. Say something."

I cleared my throat. Then, "Good evening!" The girls turned toward me. Two blondes and a brunette. When I hesitated, Tuck slapped my shoulder and whispered, "Good start. Keep going."

"Uh . . . how are you this evening?"

The one with dark hair took a step toward me. Our eyes met.

"Well, well," she said, "if it isn't my favorite co-worker." It was Juana Maria, but I hardly recognized her. Where was the peasant-girl outfit? She had on jeans and a sweater. She kicked the car tire. "That's some . . . vehicle you've got there."

"Grrrrrr." Vern gave her a dirty look.

"Hi, Juana Maria. It's a Volkswagen, 1961."

"I've seen worse." She smiled. "Not really. I was just being nice. How's it going?"

It was all the conversation we had time for. The light turned green, and Vern hit the gas. I waved. "See ya."

"See?" Tuck said from the back seat. "Friendly works."

"You know her?" Vern asked.

"We work together."

"She's hot," Tuck said.

"She insulted my car. Those are fighting words." He might drive a death trap, but it was *his* death trap.

Tuck laced his hands behind his head. "Friendly works, gentlemen. Anything you want to know about women, just ask."

He really needed to get over himself, and Vern and I spent the rest of the evening telling him so.

"Young man, there's a fly on my table." A customer at Ernesto's pointed to the insect with her eyes.

"I'll take care of it," I said. I waved a hand to get it flying. Then I snatched it out of the air. I turned to the lady and smiled as the fly buzzed in my fist. "Anything else?"

She just looked at me with her mouth open. It was a lucky grab, but she didn't need to know that. I walked outside and released it.

"Are you one of those snatch-the-pebble-from-my-hand

types?" Juana Maria asked a little later. Apparently, word had spread quickly about my fly-snatching.

"Snatch the pebble?"

"Are you some kind of martial-arts genius or something?"

I shook my head. "I had an agreement with that fly. The whole thing was staged. It's all about getting the customer to leave a big tip."

"Wow. Amazing. You speak fly?"

"Fluently."

She laughed.

I liked making her laugh, for some reason. Little dimples appeared when she smiled, which were cute as hell. Not that hell is cute, but you know what I mean.

"How did you like cruise night?" she asked.

"Pretty fun. It was my first time."

"You really need to get out more. And I recommend a new cruise vehicle."

"Not exactly a chick magnet? Is that what you're saying?"

Juana Maria shook her head. "Definitely not a chick magnet." She thought for a moment. "Hey, did you just call me a chick?"

She grimaced. Even her pissed-off face was attractive.

"Young lady? Is that better?"

"Much. Would you like another tip?"

"Sure. Lay it on me."

"When picking up girls, try not to begin with the word 'uh.'"

"Thanks. I'll work on my delivery." I made a mental note, right under "just be friendly."

The day after Christmas, Vern, Tuck, and I drove to Pasadena to work on the Rose Parade floats. It was the first road trip we'd been on since the Templin Highway and the Night of Gas. We needed a different memory.

I sat in the back as we headed south on the 101. Tuck rode shotgun (his turn) and was fiddling with the AM radio, trying to get something besides a talk show.

"How'd you hear about this, Vern?" I asked.

"My sister's friends have been doing it for years. A lot of the Rose Parade floats are put together by volunteers. They may be designed by the pros, but a lot of the finishing touches are done by volunteers. Should be fun."

Tuck finally found a top-forty station and sat back, pleased with himself. "You can thank me later," he said. It was music mixed with static, but it was better than nothing.

We got to the airplane-hangar–sized building and signed in. A fat lady covered in flower petals greeted us. "Where are you boys from?"

"Highmont Ridge," I said.

"What school?"

"Highmont Ridge High School."

She looked at her clipboard and said, "Follow me. A few of your classmates are already here. We try to group people who may know each other."

There were four or five floats being worked on in the building, each one swarming with workers. Scaffolding to reach the high places. Drills buzzing and sparks flying from arc welders behind a green plastic screen.

"You'll be working on Paul and his friend," the lady said.

We all exchanged a look. "Paul?" Vern asked.

We rounded a float, and the lady pointed. "Bunyan."

Paul Bunyan was lying down near the front of the float, in the shadow of Babe, which was mostly chicken wire that they were beginning to cover with blue paper. There was no chicken wire visible on Paul, and someone I knew was working on his shoes. Carol Ann, from math class. And I had my opening line ready.

I walked over. "Got any parallelograms on you?"

She looked up. "Hey, Elroy." She shook her head. "Nope, fresh out of parallelograms."

I turned to Vern and Tuck. "I'll work here."

Vern and Tuck went to help with the ox, and I turned back to Carol Ann. "So how can I help?"

She handed me a brown paper bag, and I looked inside. "Peppercorns," she said. "They need to be glued down one at a time."

"Tedious."

"Tell me about it."

She had on jeans and an unzipped hooded sweatshirt. Very simple, very clean.

"So how was your Christmas?" she asked. "Santa bring you anything good?" She sprayed adhesive onto Paul's foot and we began placing peppercorns. One at a time. Slow going.

"Knee pads," I said.

She turned and looked at me.

"I'm on the wrestling team."

"Really? You look more like the chess-team type."

"We don't have a chess team."

"I know," she said. "But you look the type."

We were in a public place, so it's not like I could rip my shirt off and show her, but it was fairly well documented that I had abs *and* pecs. Somehow I didn't think that chess types could say the same.

"Knee pads," she said, shaking her head. "Some Christmas present. No new pajamas? No CDs, books?"

"I got gift cards for Best Buy and Barnes & Noble."

"No pajamas?"

"I'm a guy, Carol Ann. We don't dress up to go to bed. We take our clothes *off.*"

She sprayed another patch of glue. "You don't know what you're missing."

"Leave it to girls to make sleeping so complicated."

"You don't know what you're missing," she said again. "Boys are so uncomplicated."

We kept making our way around the front of the shoe, sharing stories of home life and school. Pretty tedious work, placing peppercorns one at a time, but talking to Carol Ann was not tedious at all. This girl was growing on me.

CHAPTER SIXTEEN

Vern's legs were hanging out of the Death Trap when I rode up. I walked over and spoke to his feet. "What's happening?"

He was doing something under the dash and grunted, "New stereo. Hold on a second." He crawled out and handed me the box the stereo came in.

I checked it out—multi-disk, six speakers. The price sticker was still there. "Wow, Vern, you really busted the piggy bank."

"It's for a worthy cause, Elroy."

"Isn't that a little like putting caviar on a Wheat Thin?"

"Probably." He got back in the car and did some final tinkering. Then he pulled an iPod from his pocket and attached it. "But listen to this."

He pressed "play" and out poured crisp electric guitar and a thumping bass and drums. He turned up the volume until my ears felt like they were ready to bleed, then turned it way down and looked at me.

"Spring break, baby. The Eastern Sierra. Gotta have tunes for *that* road trip."

Okay, so maybe putting caviar on a Wheat Thin was a good idea. I had to admit, having a great sound system changed everything. Somehow the Trap was no longer the Trap. Vern had given it a soul.

And just in time for New Year's Eve. Vern and I didn't have any plans, but we knew Tuck would have something up his sleeve. That evening, when we showed up at his house, he was sitting on his front steps polishing his belt buckle. His cowboy boots were polished too, and every hair was in place—no hat.

"I had a hunch you guys would show up."

"Getting ready to go somewhere?" I asked.

"It's New Year's Eve, gentlemen. I propose we celebrate the occasion." He finished polishing his buckle and began threading the belt onto his pants. Then he stood up.

"What did you have in mind?" Vern asked.

"The Library."

I groaned. "Perusing the *Encyclopædia Britannica* is your idea of a good time?"

"No, not the public library. I mean the Library. The club."

"I thought you had to be eighteen to get in."

Tuck grabbed his wallet and flashed us his driver's license. "I have connections. Check out the birthdate." It was a fake ID, but it looked real.

"Okay, so one of us is eighteen. What about Vern and me?"

"I have that covered. Let's go."

It was my turn to ride shotgun, but I let Tuck take it. He was the guy with the plan; he could have the seat of honor. "One more thing, guys," he said.

"What's that?"

"You need to change your clothes."

Vern glanced back at me. "What's wrong with jeans and a T-shirt?"

"Not on New Year's Eve. Trust me."

Either Tuck knew what he was talking about, or he talked a big game. But he was the most experienced guy I knew outside the Second Base Club. If jeans and a T-shirt wouldn't get the job done, I'd go along.

We drove over to Vern's house, and he hopped out, calling over his shoulder, "What's the approved attire?"

"Shirt with a collar," Tuck yelled. "Better pants."

Vern came back out wearing cords and a dress shirt. His hair was wet, and he was busy trying to pull a comb through it. After a quick trip to my house, we headed to the Library. Vern's car shook from the loudness of his new stereo. It was a whole different feel from just a few days ago. We pulled into the Library parking lot. One of the bouncers was out front, checking IDs.

"Look." I pointed. "They're not going to let us in."

"Trust me," Tuck said. "I told you I have that covered."

We got out of the car, and Tuck took us around to a dark alley behind the building. "See that door?"

"What door?" Vern asked. "I just see darkness."

"There's a door down there. It opens onto the dance floor. I'll go in the main entrance"—he tapped his back pocket, fake-ID check—"and let you in. Stay near the door and dance your way in."

"Won't they see us?"

"The far side of the dance floor is completely dark." He pointed down the dark alley. "Stay near the door. Be back in a second."

Tuck left, and Vern and I crept down the dark alley, feeling our way along the walls. Couldn't see a thing. There was no way we'd find the—

"Doorknob!" Vern said suddenly.

I hit something and fell over. "Trash cans!"

I got back to my feet and felt around for Vern. "That would be my nose," he said.

Ten minutes clicked by, then another five. "Something's wrong," Vern said. "Maybe he forgot us."

My mind flashed on Tuck making out with some babe and forgetting all about his two friends. I shook the thought away. "If it wasn't going to work, he'd come and tell us."

"So what's taking—"

The door flew open. Before we could react, Tuck grabbed us and pulled us inside. The door shut behind us. Loud music. Bodies dancing all around. I moved to the rhythm, following Vern, who was following Tuck. We walk/danced across the dance floor in some kind of mini-conga. A girl behind me put her hands on my shoulders, and the train extended itself. One by one, dancers joined, alternating guy and girl. Tuck looked back at us and smiled.

After the third lap around the dance floor, the train broke up and people resumed solo dancing. Tuck pulled us to the side. "Gentlemen, enjoy your evening."

"What do you mean?" I said.

"I got you in, but I'm not here to babysit. The ladies are waiting. Let's meet up in a couple of hours. Whoever gets the most phone numbers wins." Tuck scanned the room until his eyes locked on two girls standing together. "Be good," he called over his shoulder.

"Come on, Vern," I said. "I gotta see this."

I stayed close enough to Tuck to watch, listen, and learn, but not so close that he knew he was being spied on.

"Would you like to dance?" he asked.

Two girls who had been talking to each other turned toward him. One of them said, "I don't dance."

"You don't have to dance," Tuck said.

The girl gave him a look. "But didn't you just ask—"

"You don't have to dance," Tuck said again. "Just stand there. I'll dance."

Tuck's hips gyrated to the beat of the music. His feet shuffled. He did stylish things with his hands and arms, but his eyes stayed on hers. And he never stopped smiling. The girl couldn't help smiling back. After a while she began to dance. Tuck gestured to the dance floor. "I'm Tuck. Shall we?"

"Sarah," she said, following him out onto the floor.

Vern looked at me. "Okay, I'm impressed."

"Yeah," I said. "Amazing."

But somehow we realized that would only work for Tuck. We would have to find our own way. Vern said, "So what do we do now?"

"We get a grog and think it over."

"A grog?"

"Something to drink."

We made our way through the crowd toward the bar. On the way, we checked out the joint. The Library looked like a library. The four walls were bookshelves that reached the ceiling. A spiral staircase led to a balcony, which overlooked the dance floor. People were everywhere, upstairs and down—and all the girls were eighteen or older. Oh my!

I slapped my hand on the bar and said, "Root beer."

"Easy, Wyatt Earp." The bartender pointed to the soda

fountain stuffed away in a corner. "Serve yourself. What size drink would you like?"

"Medium."

Vern ordered the same.

We got our drinks and clinked paper cups. "To second base and beyond," I said.

"Sounds good to me."

I scanned the room, looking for Tuck. He was out on the dance floor with a different girl. He was an okay dancer, but what made him stand out, I think, was that he never stopped smiling and he looked his partner in the eye.

"Where'd he learn this stuff?" Vern asked.

"Exactly. He could open a school."

We stood there watching as if it was Michael Jordan putting on a clinic. Sometimes Tuck would grab the girl he was dancing with and they'd slow-dance briefly, right in the middle of a fast song. Sometimes he'd lean in and say something and the girl would laugh or smile.

"Something tells me we're not going to win the phone-number competition," I said.

"Yeah." Vern tossed his empty drink cup in the trash and turned to me. "Come on, Elroy. Want to mingle?"

"You mean like actually talk to some girls?"

"You mean women."

"Oh my!"

"Exactly."

We threaded our way through the crowd, trying not to look too eager. Some girls were already paired up with guys. Either they came with dates or they were in the middle of seducing or being seduced.

We made a lap of the room, then another.

"One of us is going to have to speak up," Vern said.

"You mean like ask someone to dance?"

"Yes."

I remembered what Tuck had said on cruise night. Just be friendly. If you can't be witty or charming, just be friendly. Made a whole lot of sense.

I spotted two girls standing together. I cracked my knuckles. "Okay, I'm going in." I walked up to one of the girls and blurted it out. I forced myself to say the words. "Excuse me, but would you like to dance?"

They turned toward me. Seconds ticked by. I tried not to read too much into their expressions. More seconds ticked by. And then one of them shrugged and said, "Sure, why not."

I gave her my arm and led her out onto the dance floor as a song was coming to the end and the place fell quiet. The DJ came on the microphone and said, "Let's slow things down a tad."

Crap! A slow song.

I turned to face the girl, and she put her hands around my neck and moved in close. My hands immediately went to her waist. And it was a great waist! We circled once, twice. Her hips moved toward mine, but mine moved back. Couldn't let her know what I was thinking. It was like the old A-frame hug, only it was prolonged and we were twirling. Our upper torsos were touching but our hips (my hips) were a mile away.

I glanced over at Tuck, who had his full body mashed up against some girl. He was looking right at me and making a face, putting his palms together as if to say, "Move in, Elroy. Let her know how you really feel."

I couldn't bring myself to do it.

We kept dancing, and when the song ended, I thanked the girl and she walked off. I didn't even get her name. "I'm Elroy,"

I mumbled as the music changed back to a fast song and all the clinging couples broke apart and started dancing individually.

I walked over to Vern. "You did it," he said, then added, "I never saw two people dance so close together and so far apart at the same time."

"I know." But, like he said, I did it. I spoke up. I danced. That was more than he'd done. I scanned the room, spotted a girl standing alone, got behind Vern, and shoved him forward. "You're on, Vern. Make me proud."

CHAPTER SEVENTEEN

Tuck won the phone-number contest hands down. He sat in the back seat of the Trap on the way home, plugging the numbers into his cell phone. He had seven numbers in all. Vern and I came up empty.

"You know how some companies sell their mailing lists?" Tuck asked.

"Yeah, why?"

"Just thinking. Anyone want to buy a hot girl's phone number?"

"Get over yourself, Tuck," I said.

"I'm trying. It ain't easy."

Vern drove us home, Tuck first, then me. Mom was sitting on my couch/bed reading when I walked in.

"How was it?" she asked.

I shrugged. "Fine. I danced." I didn't tell her I danced nine feet apart from my partner.

"Fast or slow?" Mom asked.

"Slow."

She put down her book. "Please don't tell me you did the A-frame dance."

"Okay, I won't tell you."

"Why do boys do that?"

"Trust me, Mom. You don't want to know."

"I suppose not." She grabbed her book again and turned a page. "Though I do have my suspicions."

I did twelve and a half pull-ups on my pull-up tree, which was my PB (personal best), then sat on the front steps of the Airstream, waiting for Vern. It was our first day back to school after Christmas break, and it finally felt like winter. In southern California that meant you had to wear a sweatshirt for at least half the day.

Vern pulled up, and I got in. My mom was at the door with her fingers in her ears, shaking her head. She mouthed something to us.

"What did she say?" Vern asked as he shoved the car in gear and we took off down Casitas Pass.

"I think she wants you to acquire a muffler at your earliest convenience."

"Yeah, I was thinking about that. Might be able to hear the stereo better."

My school schedule for the spring semester was exactly the same as the fall, with one notable exception. I signed up for weight training for my sixth-period elective. I thought adding a little more muscle might help my chances on the wrestling mat, and it couldn't hurt in the girl department. I'd continue doing pull-ups on my backyard oak tree, but I wanted something a little more formal. .

So, for sixth period, I headed to the weight room, which was just off the boys' locker room. There were two girls in the class who looked like Russian shotputters. The rest were guys. The instructor, Mr. Phelps, looked a lot like Coach Grogan, without the mangled ears.

"The key to lifting weights, gentlemen"—he turned to the two girls—"and ladies, is doing the exercises correctly and safely. I want you each to grab a partner. You will be training with that person for the rest of the year."

The two girls immediately paired up. So did the guys. I was left standing alone.

Mr. Phelps looked at me. "Why don't you join in with—"

And that's when Sampson Teague showed up. He walked into the room looking like the god he was. "Sorry, Coach," he said. "It won't happen again."

"Perfect," Mr. Phelps said. "Now we've got an even number. Sampson, you'll train with—"

"Elroy," I said.

"Elroy."

Sampson came over and slapped me on the back way too hard. "How's it going?"

"It's going okay," I told him. I looked around the room. Maybe there was someone hiding in the corner that I could pair up with—anyone but Sampson. But the corners were empty. I was stuck with the potential-girlfriend stealer.

Coach Phelps demonstrated a few exercises—curls, keeping his elbows at his sides; shoulder presses, not coming too low and never locking his elbows. "We're working the muscle, not the joint."

The class then broke up and began training. Sampson walked over to the dumbbells on the rack against the wall and grabbed a few. "Tell me if I'm doing this right, Elroy."

Did I have to?

Sampson curled the weights while I watched, one arm, then the other. Then he looked at me for feedback. I didn't say a word.

"Well?" he asked. "Good form or not?"

I forced myself to speak. "Slow it down. Keep your upper body still."

After his set, he handed the weights to me. I curled them once and stopped.

"What's the matter?"

I put the dumbbells down. "A little too heavy for me. Need to go down a size."

When I finished my set, we went to the leg machine, then on to shoulder presses. We were both sweating and breathing hard by the end of class, but I kept my comments to a minimum. I was Sampson's partner because the coach put us together, not out of choice. I still had hopes that someone new would join the class so I could dump him. Let him know what it feels like to be rejected.

Sampson and I walked out of the weight room together and headed for the locker room.

"Thanks, Elroy," he said to me. "You're a good person to work out with."

Whatever, dude.

CHAPTER EIGHTEEN

My match against Aquinas was some kind of fluke. Maybe it was because at the time I thought it was my one and only match of the season and I gave it my all. Maybe it was because my parents were sitting in the stands. I'm not sure. But I lost the next five matches, all of them JV. It wasn't pretty. My only consolation was that no girls my age were there to witness it. Or not many, anyway. One of the teams we went up against actually had cheerleaders. Imagine being on your back and hearing a bunch of female voices chanting, "Pin, pin, pin, pin!"

Total humiliation. But at least the girls weren't from Highmont. And Vern didn't make the event more public by writing about it. He came to the matches and wrote further articles, just not about me. Mike Thomas and Todd Waylan, yes. Me, no.

I didn't mind being anonymous.

"Call me Mr. Studly," Vern said as he sat down beside me in the quad.

"Excuse me?" I said.

"Mr. Studly. Go ahead, say it."

"And why would I do this?"

"Because Vern Zuckman was just asked to the backwards dance." He looked at me with his I'm-not-kidding-you look and nodded. "Yep, Carmen Medina asked me."

I just looked at him, not yet ready to believe. After all, this was Vern Zuckman I was talking to.

"Remember I told you that most of the *Highmont Herald*'s staff were girls?"

"Yeah."

"The plan worked. Carmen is one of the photographers. We've been covering gymnastics and wrestling. She takes the pictures—I write the words."

"And she just came out and asked you?"

Vern nodded. "I wasn't even doing anything, just working. Carmen is at least a seven. Don't you think?"

"I'd say so." Carmen wasn't bad at all. This was serious. Vern had a date and I didn't. I'd better start throwing out some serious charming vibes.

Tuck showed up a few minutes later, and Vern shared his big news.

"Way to go." He pulled his Skoal can from his back pocket and offered us a mint. "Take two, Vern. You deserve it."

Two days later, Tuck was asked to the dance. I was still dateless. And my charming vibes didn't seem to be working. I'd have to be more direct.

I walked into math class and sat down across from Carol Ann with an exaggerated sigh. When she ignored it, I did it again. She fumbled in her purse and handed me some kind of inhaler. "Here," she said. "I have asthma too."

"No, it's not that. I'm just worried, is all." I didn't know what my worried face looked like, but I tried to conjure one.

"What about?"

"I haven't been asked to the backwards dance yet." I paused for effect, letting it sink in, then, "Who are you going with?"

She laughed. "Nice try, Elroy."

Crap! So much for being direct. Mrs. Dumar passed out a worksheet, but I couldn't concentrate. Under every triangle I drew a half-circle, turning each into someone wearing a dunce cap. I kept my head down and continued to doodle, avoiding eye contact with Carol Ann. I didn't want to be laughed at again. I added bodies to the faces and put one of the dunces on a skateboard with—

A folded-up piece of paper landed on my desk. I opened it and stared at the words written on it.

> Would you like to go to the backwards
> dance with me, Elroy?
>
> Carol Ann

I glanced across the aisle, and Carol Ann was looking right at me. Just when you think your charming vibes have gone into hibernation, something like this happens. I wrote a big "YES!" beneath the skateboarding dunce and held it up.

"Elroy, is that something you'd like to share with the class?" Mrs. Dumar growled.

"Uh . . . no," I said. I flipped the paper over and began working the problems on the back side. I couldn't help smiling. I was going to the backwards dance after all. Carol Ann was at least as cute as Carmen Medina.

After class, Carol Ann and I walked out together. "So how does this work?" I asked her. "Do you pick me up? Do you pay for dinner?"

"It's like a normal date, Elroy. The boy does everything. The girl just pops the question to set it in motion."

"You mean I drive? I pay for dinner?"

"Pretty much." She smiled. "I love being a girl."

I met up with Vern and Tuck. "I'm in," I told them.

"You're in?" Vern said. "You don't look it."

"You're in what?" Tuck asked.

I held out my hand. "Two mints, please."

Tuck and Vern exchanged a look.

"I'm going to the backwards dance!"

Vern slapped me a high-five.

Tuck reached for the Skoal can. "So who's the unlucky girl?"

"Carol Ann Tassner."

Tuck and Vern exchanged another look. "Not bad, Elroy," Vern said. "You two going by bike?"

"Good question." Transportation was a problem. I didn't have a car. Getting to the dance wouldn't be easy.

"You're going to double-date with Vern?" Mom was pretty happy that I'd been asked to the dance, but not as impressed with Vern's mode of transportation.

"Yes, we're taking the Death Trap."

"But it's so loud. You know, dating is all about conversation. You won't be able to hear a thing."

"Conversation is highly overrated," I told her. "We'll think of something else to do."

Mom gave me a raised eyebrow. When I didn't respond, she raised the other one.

"I'm kidding." I wasn't, but she didn't have to know that. Something *else* sounded pretty good to me.

That night, before bed, I did a serious pimple-check. I found one on my chin, but it wasn't enormous. Not one of those pinch-it-and-it-hits-the-mirror types. This one petered out halfway there. The rest of my face was immaculate—except for a few mat burns. But I was hoping they would make me look rugged, in a battle-wound kind of way.

I went to bed feeling good. I had a date with a pretty girl, who'd asked *me*. Maybe I had put the idea in her head. Maybe I had to foot the bill. But she did the asking. She wanted me.

Kind of.

CHAPTER NINETEEN

On the night of the dance, we went to a place called Mickey Moose for dinner, where I spent my time making intelligent conversation and touching knees with Carol Ann. She didn't flinch. I took this as a good sign.

When she and Carmen got up to use the bathroom, Vern said, "So what's the NP, Elroy?"

"NP?"

"Nooky Plan."

"Not sure." I thought for a moment. "Be charming, dance our butts off, and see if they want to go park after the dance?"

Vern nodded. "Sounds about right. Here they come. Smile, Elroy."

I have to admit, smiling came easy. And I positioned my knee just so.

After dinner we drove to the dance, arriving fashionably late, as Vern put it. We didn't want to be the first ones there, or the last. The gym was packed when we got there. Most of the lights were off, and a mirrored ball was suspended from the ceiling. I turned to Carol Ann. "Would you like some punch?"

"Sure."

Vern and I made our way through the crowd to the punch bowl, where Mr. Phelps was keeping an eye out for potential punch-spikers. I held up a couple of fingers. "Two, please."

Someone squeezed my biceps. I turned to face Sampson Teague. "Impressive," he said. "You must lift weights or something." He held out his hand. "How's it going, Elroy?"

"Great," I said. "You clean up nice."

"Don't I, though." He walked off waving his hand behind him, a girl on his arm. She was not Marisa.

Who dumped who? I scanned the crowd for Marisa as Vern and I grabbed our drinks and headed back to Carol Ann and Carmen. No sign of her.

Vern said, "So you're pals with Mr. Second Base Club now?"

"We just work out together."

We joined our dates and wandered through the crowd. I gulped down my drink and tossed the empty cup in a trash can. "Would you like to dance, Carol Ann?"

"I would."

She took my arm, and we headed to the middle of the crowded dance floor and began moving to the music. Tuck was already there, belt buckle gleaming under the mirrored ball, dancing way too close for a fast song. I had to admire his confidence. I remembered some of his moves from the night at the Library and tried to imitate them—keeping eye contact with Carol Ann, smiling. She smiled back. The song ended and another one began. We stayed on the floor.

Vern joined us a few minutes later. Turned out that Carmen belonged to a church that didn't believe in dancing. This was her chance. She kept Vern on the floor all night long.

Carol Ann and I took time out to wander, mingle with some of her friends, get more punch. But not Vern. Once Carmen got him out on the floor, he never left it. Every time I saw him, he had less on—coat and tie gone, sleeves rolled up. He was sweating pretty heavily by the time the dance was over. "The things I do for nooky," he whispered to me as we headed out.

"You wish," I said.

He held up two crossed fingers. "I do."

The question was, did they? Was the evening over, or had it just begun? We walked out to the Trap and got in. Vern said, "You ladies want to go for a drive?"

No answer—the longest pause in history.

Vern looked over his shoulder at me. Carmen and Carol Ann exchanged a glance.

"I'd better get home," Carol Ann said finally. "My dad can get weird sometimes."

Carmen nodded. "Yeah, me too."

Crap! No, this was worse than crap. "Shit!" I said under my breath. At least I thought it was under my breath.

Carol Ann nudged me. "What was that?"

Vern started the car, and we headed out of the parking lot. I let my knee wander over to Carol Ann's side. There was still a chance that this date could end in a kiss. My knee would have to make it happen.

Vern drove to Carol Ann's house and parked on the street, a tree blocking the view of the front door. Good ol' Vern. He was smart enough to know that what came next was private.

We got out of the car, and I walked her to the door. I expected her dad to pop out any minute and give me the evil eye. When he didn't I said, "I had a great time, Carol Ann. Thanks for asking me."

"I did too." She laughed. "Thanks for getting me to ask you."

"I know. I kind of cheated."

"I might have asked you anyway. You just made it easier."

"Hey, whatever works."

"Exactly. I didn't have to work as hard."

Now what? Was this when I made my move? After all, our knees were somewhat familiar with one another.

"So . . . I . . . uh . . ." I stepped forward, head tilting to one side, lips parting slightly, and—

Carol Ann stiff-armed me. Arms extended, one on my shoulder, the other on my neck. I tried to say something but all that came out was *Aaaack!*

She let go. "This is not that kind of date, Elroy."

Tell that to our knees! While I was adjusting my Adam's apple, she opened the door and went inside. "Good night."

CHAPTER TWENTY

"**S**o what's eating you, Elroy?"

It was pretty slow the following afternoon at Ernesto's. Juana Maria and I were sitting in a booth, eating tacos and folding napkins.

"Hello? Earth to Elroy." She waved a hand in my face.

Needless to say, I hadn't slept the night before. I kept playing the scene over in my head—me leaning in for the kiss, Carol Ann stiff-arming my neck. *Aaaack!* How humiliating. Now I had two girls I needed to avoid, and both of them were in my math class.

Juana Maria snapped her fingers and I looked up.

"You look like you haven't slept in nine days."

"Had a date last night," I admitted. "Didn't end the way I wanted it to."

Juana Maria put down the taco she was about to bite into, pushed her plate to one side, and plopped her head on her hands, elbows on the table. "Okay, you have my attention. Tell me everything."

"I just did. I had a date. It didn't end well. End of story."

"Details, Elroy. I'm a girl. We like details."

I thought about whether or not I should say anything. Mom couldn't get me to spill the beans, but there was something about Juana Maria. Her eyes didn't bore through me like my mother's. Maybe it was because she was my age. I don't know, but I felt that I could talk to her, that I *wanted* to talk to her. I began to tell her the story—the whole story. Not just about Carol Ann shutting me down, but about my brief tutoring gig with Marisa, sitting on her porch, and now working out with the guy who stole her from me.

"Hold on." Juana Maria reached across the table and squeezed my biceps. "You lift weights? I thought something was going on. I thought it was because of wrestling."

"Well, that too."

"And how's that going, the wrestling?"

"Not sure. I get beat up a lot. I'm sticking with it because my parents come to matches. They're separated, but if I keep wrestling it forces them to spend time together. Kind of weird, huh? Joining a sport for all the wrong reasons."

"Doing something for someone else is never the wrong reason," she said.

"Well, initially I just joined to impress girls."

"You think girls like tweaked ears?"

"You mean they don't?"

Juana Maria laughed. "Good. You're fraternizing. Feeling better?"

I nodded. "Yes, I am." Talking to her helped. I *did* feel better. Mom couldn't get it out of me, but somehow Juana Maria did.

"Seriously, Elroy, don't you think it's exhausting?"

"What is?"

"Spending all your time and energy being someone other than yourself." She let that sink in. Then she got up from the table. "Break time's over. We've got customers." She left me sitting there.

I cleared the table and wiped it down before joining her.

"Go ahead and say it, Elroy."

"Say what?"

"I'm smarter than I look."

"Actually, you look kind of smart."

All afternoon I kept thinking about what she'd said about my spending all my time and energy being something other than myself. So far it hadn't gotten me anywhere.

On Monday, Sampson didn't show up for sixth-period weight training. I'd been pretty unresponsive for the first week or two, but he was never anything but friendly toward me. Eventually, I let my guard down. We'd been getting along, working out hard, challenging each other to push it a little. But spilling my guts to Juana Maria kind of brought back the pain of being dumped, so I was okay with not having a partner.

Coach Phelps had me work out with the dumbbells, a couple of guys named Rich and Charlie, who spent the entire class recapping *Saturday Night Live* skits as we worked our way through the weight circuit. I was glad for the comic relief. It kept my mind from replaying Carol Ann's stiff-arm.

And I got a pretty decent workout.

Coach Grogan had called off practice. Someone said that he was having too much fun in Las Vegas, and he didn't want to come home just yet. I took a shower, dried off, and wrapped a towel around my waist. On the way back to my locker, I noticed that the locker with the list of names from the Second Base Club stood wide open. No one was around. I had to take a look. Sampson Teague was still in the lead with twenty points. Jerry, the tight end from the football team, was in second with sixteen. I read down the list. A few guys with fifteen, one with twelve, and a four-way tie at ten.

I kissed a girl for nine seconds on her porch, and now I wasn't even getting that far. What did they know that I didn't?

"Ping-Pong tournament scores," came a voice over my shoulder.

I turned around. It was the guy I'd seen announcing the list back when Sampson was just barely into double digits.

"In case you're wondering," he said. He had a towel around his waist and one over his shoulder. His arms were about as big as my thighs. "You always read stuff in other people's lockers?"

"Kind of a hobby," I said.

He almost laughed.

By this time a few other Second Base Club members were standing around us. One of them was Jerry. How was this guy in second place? He was about six foot five and had hair sprouting everywhere below the neck.

The owner of the locker pointed to the score sheet. "I was just telling our friend here about the Ping-Pong scores."

"The what?" Jerry said, not taking his eyes off me.

"Ping-Pong. You know, the secret Ping-Pong tournament." I think I saw him wink.

Finally, Jerry caught on. "Yes. The Ping-Pong tournament." He gestured to the list. "And I bet you thought Sampson just played football."

"A secret Ping-Pong tournament?" I said. "Why is it secret?"

"Because it is," Jerry said. "And there's no room for more players, in case you're wondering."

"Just asking," I said. "Because if I didn't know better I'd say this had something to do with girls."

Jerry shot a look to a few of his friends.

"Elroy knows all," I said, backing up a bit.

Jerry slammed his fist against one of the lockers. "Maybe you need to mind your own business. I said the tournament is closed."

"The Ping-Pong tournament?"

"That's right. The Ping-Pong tournament."

I backed up some more and raised an open hand, feeling the hair stand up on the back of my neck. "Hey, no problem." I tromped down the aisle to my locker and sat down, heart beating like crazy. No sense getting beat up over . . . Ping-Pong. I put on my clothes quickly and went out to the parking lot. Vern was waiting for me.

"Ping-Pong?" Vern said when I told him the story.

"Yeah, can you believe it?"

"And now they know that you know. Maybe you should have kept your mouth shut."

"Maybe," I said. I had to admit, Jerry kind of scared me. He looked at me with dead eyes, like he'd kick my ass for no reason at all, for the sheer joy of seeing another human being bleed. Plus, he was huge. I guess it was the front-door episode with Carol Ann, the rejection, the humiliation. I was curious about the Second Base Club. These were the guys getting somewhere with the opposite sex. I could see how girls might go for Sampson, but Jerry was just this big guy covered with hair.

My only consolation was that Vern wasn't doing any better. His date with Carmen ended in a handshake.

"Maybe we could start our own Second Base Club," Vern said as he turned onto Casitas Pass. "You, me, and Tuck."

I thought about this, then looked at Vern and shook my head. "Nah. Tuck would be in double digits immediately, and you and I would still be in the same boat."

"True. Tuck has it going on, and he does it without being an asshole."

"Exactly."

Vern pulled to a stop in front of the Airstream and I got out. "See you tomorrow."

I went inside, dropped my books on the couch, grabbed my guitar, and began picking a random tune, going over the events of the day.

The phone rang, and I answered it. "Hello?"

"Turn on Channel Seven." It was Vern.

"What's on Channel Seven?"

"You gotta see it. Turn it on." He paused. "You there yet?"

"Hold on." I turned on the TV and scrolled down to seven. It was some kind of rock concert, an ancient group that had been big in the sixties. A bunch of old guys, but they could rock. The cameras flashed on the audience. The ones near the stage were mostly women. They were going wild and tossing something at the performers.

"What's that they're throwing?" I asked.

"Underwear. Are you seeing this? They're throwing their underwear!" Vern was more excited than I'd seen him in a while. Actually, I was hearing him.

"Wow."

"I know. It's like the ultimate Second Base Club."

I watched the mayhem continue. Women of all ages were throwing their underwear at these geezers, just because they made music. The world just wasn't fair—that's all there was to it. I was no geezer. I could do twelve pull-ups. I had pecs and abs, for crying out loud. I beat a varsity wrestler from Aquinas. This was—

Vern's words banged around in my head. A rock-and-roll band, the ultimate Second Base Club.

"You play guitar, right, Elroy?"

"I do."

"I could get a bass." Vern paused. "Do you know anyone who can play drums?"

"I saw a drum kit in Tuck's garage."

"Perfect!"

Yeah, it was perfect. If geezers could do it, so could we.

CHAPTER TWENTY-ONE

On Saturday, we headed over to South Coast Music, the largest guitar store in the Tri-Counties. They had tons of basses. Vern and I browsed, not really knowing what we were looking for, although you-get-what-you-pay-for was always a good rule of thumb to fall back on. And the price range was huge.

"Might have to break the piggy bank on this one," I told Vern, fingering some of the price tags. "You got a price in mind?"

"Four hundred."

I whistled. First his car stereo, now the bass guitar. Either he had saved every dime he earned at Perry's Pretzels or—

Vern flashed his dad's credit card.

I must have had that where'd-you-get-the-dough look.

"As long as I take lessons, the old man will foot the bill."

"In that case"—I started flipping price tags—"check out this baby. . . . Eleven hundred. No, wait. Here's one for fifteen."

He shook his head. "Four hundred's my limit."

"Doesn't he know it's for a good cause?"

"Guess not. And I can't exactly tell him." Vern strapped on a bass and plucked a string. Then he started in on "Mary Had a Little Lamb."

"Impressed?"

"Kind of. Can you play for real?"

"No. That's why I need lessons."

A salesman stood nearby, giving us a hard look. He had on a dress shirt and tie, hair past his shoulders. Obviously, this was just a day job.

"I'll take it," Vern said.

The hard look vanished.

We went to the counter, and Vern paid and asked about lessons. A flyer on the counter caught my attention:

BATTLE OF THE BANDS
Highmont Ridge Fairgrounds
April 7
1st place — $500

I elbowed Vern and pointed to the flyer. "We should enter," I said. "If we win—"

"We'll get nailed with underwear?"

"Exactly."

We drove directly from the guitar store to Tuck's house. I was hoping the drum kit I'd seen in his garage had been doing more than collecting dust. Tuck was out front mowing the lawn when we pulled up. He had his shirt off, and I couldn't help noticing— he had better pecs than me! Damn.

"Gentlemen." He shut off the engine and wiped his face with the shirt tied around his waist.

"We're starting a rock-and-roll band," I said.

"To meet girls," Vern added.

Tuck put his shirt on and walked over. "A rock-and-roll band to meet girls. Okay, I can see the logic. But I already told you how to meet girls—just be friendly."

"We need more help," I said. "Haven't you noticed? Rock and roll might give us a boost."

"I *have* noticed," Tuck said. "You do need a little extra something." He gestured to his garage, which had the door up. "Why don't we step into my office."

We followed him into the garage. The drum kit sat in the corner. I checked it for dust and rust. I didn't see any. "You play the drums?" I asked.

He nodded, grabbing some folding chairs for us to sit on. "Been playing off and on for years."

Vern looked at me and smiled. "Perfect. I just bought a bass, and Elroy will play guitar."

"A three-man band?" Tuck asked.

"It'll work," I told him. "We don't need a keyboard player."

Tuck was slowly coming around, but I could tell he needed a little more to make him commit. After all, meeting girls was not an issue for him. He was wired for confidence. I told him about Battle of the Bands, about playing at the fairgrounds, about the five-hundred-dollar prize. Vern added the bit about the geezers pelted with feminine underwear.

"Panties," Tuck said. "Guys wear underwear; girls wear panties. Learn the terminology."

"Okay, panties." It sounded better, for some reason.

"Besides, those geezers are called the Rolling Stones. Heard of them? They're kind of famous."

"They may be famous, but they're butt-ugly." I lifted my shirt and pointed to my stomach. "Check this out, Tuck. I have abs and I'm being ignored."

"So what do we call ourselves?" Tuck asked. "Tuck's Band has a nice ring to it."

We tossed about a few names, but nothing stuck. I wasn't worried. The main thing was that Tuck was willing to join us. We had no idea if we could make music, but at least we were willing to try.

That night, I Googled band names. There didn't seem to be any rhyme or reason to them. Let's face it, The Beatles is a pretty crappy name. It was their music that made them stand out. They could have called themselves Smelly Socks. Wouldn't have mattered. They would still have taken the world by storm.

I kept researching band names. In the old days there were a lot of bands named for animals and bugs—Animals, Monkees, Crickets. Bands named for cities—Chicago, Boston—or countries—America. Even states—Kansas. Or just plain weird stuff, like Toad the Wet Sprocket, or Hootie and the Blowfish, Death Cab for Cutie, Red Jumpsuit Apparatus. Like I said, no rhyme or reason. It was the band members that mattered. It was about the music they made.

On Monday morning, the three of us met up in the quad to talk it over. I brought my list. They brought theirs. Just like the band names I'd Googled, our suggestions were all over the place: Atomic Slugs, Hubcap Transition, Unibrow, Kneecap Repairmen, Yellow Snow. Nothing clicked.

"I still say The Mayfield Boys sounds awesome."

Vern and I shot him down.

We kept going. The Dingbats, Dipstick, Rustic Door Knob, Hot Dogs with Mustard. It was more than a brainstorm, it was a tornado. We considered everything.

"How about The Kitchen Sink?" I offered.

"The Lawnmowers?" Tuck asked.

And then Vern said it. "We could called ourselves Templin Highway."

We all stopped and looked at one another.

"Templin Highway?" I repeated. "You mean like Templin Highway and the Night of Gas?"

"I'm still trying to forget that experience," Tuck said.

But the more we thought about it, the more we talked it over, the more we realized Vern had come up with the perfect name. Templin Highway. It grew on us quickly. We knew we couldn't call ourselves anything else. Our band had a name. It was time to start practicing.

I went home and tried my hand at writing a song.

> *Look at my biceps*
> *Ain't they pumpin'*
> *Does it make you feel like jumpin'*
> *My bones?*

Well, Marvin Gaye came right out and said "Let's Get It On." Isn't that just another way of saying, "Please, jump my bones at your earliest convenience?" But maybe it would be better to be less direct. I started again.

> *I saw you the other day*
> *Wish I knew how to make you stay*
> *Wanted to call you up on the phone*
> *Wanted to tell you to jump my bones*
> *At your earliest convenience*
> *At your earliest conveeeeenience!*

Crap! I did it again. I had to find a way to keep bone jumping out of the song. The folks at Battle of the Bands might not like it. Maybe I should stay off the girl subject altogether. I looked at my life for inspiration. It didn't help. My life was all about girls. Becoming a tutor was all about girls. My job at Ernesto's was all about girls. So was wrestling. And now I was in a band for the same reason. Okay, maybe my life wasn't the best place for inspiration. Or maybe I just had to focus on romance instead of sex.

I crumpled up the piece of paper where I'd written the two bone-jumping songs and began again. I kept the beginning of the last song and went from there.

> *I saw you the other day*
> *Didn't know how to make you stay*
> *Especially when you stiff-armed me*
> *I knew you just wanted to get away*
> *Because I'm a geek*
> *I'm a geeee-eeek!*

That wasn't the half of it. I was also a shitty songwriter.

I threw the song away and went outside behind the trailer to my oak tree. I jumped up and grabbed the branch where I did my pull-ups. This time I just hung there, feeling the rough bark dig into my hands. I hung on for a long time, thinking. I didn't do a single pull-up. Then I went back inside, put on my running shoes, and took off into the hills behind the Airstream.

The trail led up into the canyon. We usually ended wrestling practice with a two-mile run around the track. Running in the canyon felt better. I followed the trail for about a mile, spooking lizards and rabbits, and a few unseen creatures hiding in the grass. After a while, the trail gave way to a creek bed littered with boulders. I slowed down a bit to avoid twisting an ankle. The creek bed eventually became a dry waterfall, and I pressed on, climbing the thing as if it was part of my workout.

At the top of the waterfall, I stopped and took in the view. Highmont Ridge spread out before me, and beyond it the blue waters of the Pacific. Right then the words came to me.

> *Highmont Ridge is the place to be*
> *Along the coast on the Pacific Sea*
> *Where the weather's fine, all year long*
> *And the girls are finer, but don't get me wrong*
> *'Cause I'm a man who's on a journey*
> *And I need more than a Ping-Pong tourney*
> *To make me discover what I can be*
> *Here in Highmont, on the Pacific Sea*

Well, at least I didn't mention bone jumping. Battle of the Bands was on April 7. I had until then to become a better songwriter.

CHAPTER TWENTY-TWO

"**Y**ou're in a band?" Juana Maria searched my face to see if I was lying.

"I'm in a band," I said.

"Really?"

The dinner rush was over, and we were catching our breath. I was hoping for no late-night eaters. But you never knew. People craved tacos at all hours.

"Yep," I told her. "Want my autograph?"

"What's the band called?"

The front door swung open, and in walked Jerry from the Second Base Club. He was with a few other guys I'd seen lingering around the locker room, all members of the secret Ping-Pong organization.

"Three for dinner?" I said, forcing cheerfulness into my voice, faking a smile.

It took Jerry a while to recognize me, what with my fluffy Mexican shirt and all. When he did, his eyes bored into me. I returned the stare. "Would you like a booth?" I asked, again cheerfully.

Another group walked through the open door. Juana Maria grabbed three menus, gestured for Jerry and his friends to follow her, and led them to the far end of the restaurant. I seated the next group.

"What was that all about?" she asked a little later.

"What was what about?"

"Those three guys. They looked at you like you just killed their mother."

"You really want to know?" I asked. Part of me didn't want to tell her—Vern, Tuck, and I were the only ones who knew about the Second Base Club—but part of me did. I can't explain it. Juana Maria had a way of getting things out of me.

"Kind of," she said.

Before I could stop myself, my mouth fell open and started talking. "There's this secret society at my school. They call themselves the Second Base Club. A bunch of jocks who keep score of their sexual exploits."

She let out a small gasp, like she didn't believe her ears. "Are you serious?"

I nodded. "I kind of eavesdropped a few times. Anyway, one of the three that you just seated seems to have it in for me. I think he suspects that I know."

"Second Base Club?" Juana Maria made a face like she was about to puke. "What a bunch of losers."

About an hour later, Jerry and his two cronies left, but Jerry made a point of grabbing a mint from the podium where I was standing and giving me another hard look. Then he walked away.

I couldn't help myself. "Good luck playing Ping-Pong." He

didn't turn around, so I added, "And good luck with the Second Base Club. Second place ain't bad."

He stopped and turned around. If looks could kill, I'd have been a goner.

"Do you have a death wish, Elroy?" Ernesto's was finally empty, and Juana Maria and I were doing our end-of-the-night routine—filling salt and pepper shakers, wrapping silverware, sweeping the entry.

"Think I should have kept my mouth shut?"

"Yes, I do. Not all people are sane. You don't know what he's capable of."

I hadn't thought of that. I just couldn't stand being stared at by a gonad named Jerry when I hadn't done anything but show a little curiosity about a list posted in someone's locker.

"You better watch your back." Juana Maria gave me a worried look.

"Don't tell me Juana Maria is concerned for Elroy's safety."

She shook her head, but the worried look didn't budge. "I'm concerned with *Elwood's* safety. Seriously, he looked kind of crazy to me. Plus, he's what I'd call extra large."

"Thanks," I told her. He was extra large. And extra hairy. "I'll be careful. I travel in groups. A murder can't take place if everyone's looking."

Ernesto popped out of his office and gave us his "scoot" gesture. I grabbed my sweatshirt and walked Juana Maria to her car. The parking lot was empty, no lingering Second Base Club members. I did a quick scan, just in case they were lying in wait. The place was deserted.

Juana Maria chirped her car alarm, then stopped and faced me. "You never told me the name of your band."

"Templin Highway."

"Templin Highway?" she asked.

"It's better than Rustic Door Knob or Hubcap Transition."

"I don't know. I kind of like Hubcap Transition."

"Me too. That was my second choice." I grabbed the handle and opened her car door. She gave me a smile, and I felt my face go hot. I was such a sucker for a hot girl's smile, especially in close quarters.

"You polite guy, you," she said as she stepped in.

"I try," I told her. But the funny thing was, I wasn't trying at all. I never tried with Juana Maria. She was the only girl who got to see the real Elroy.

She closed the car door and started the engine. I couldn't help staring. Those dark eyes and hair were . . . And that smile. Wow.

She rolled down her window. "What is it?"

"Oops. Was I staring?" I could feel my facing growing hot again.

"Kind of."

"It's a compliment. Trust me."

"I know." She pulled away slowly and called back, "And I do."

"Am I the only one who thinks this should be all about playing great music?" Tuck asked.

I looked at Vern. "What is he saying, Vern? Is he speaking English?"

"Not sure. Illogical English, maybe."

I nodded. "Being in a band should be about the music? I never heard of such a thing."

"You guys are pathetic," Tuck said. He pulled the Skoal can from his back pocket and grabbed a mint.

We were in his garage for our first practice. Vern on bass, Tuck on drums, me on guitar. Everything was plugged in and ready to go. The problem was how to begin. And the bigger question regarding Battle of the Bands—should we cover old classics, or should we make up our own?

"I agree, Tuck," I said finally. "It should be all about the music."

Vern looked at me in horror. "What are you saying?"

"And," I added, "the better we get at playing music, the better our chances in the girl department."

"Whew!" Vern wiped a hand across his forehead. "You had me worried."

"Right." Tuck twirled a drumstick. "We focus on the music and all good things will come." All good things came to him, anyway. "So what's our first song?"

We kicked around a few ideas and decided in the end that if we were a band that was all about the music, then, do or die, we'd play original songs for Battle of the Bands. Now we just needed a song—or two.

Tuck disappeared inside the house and came back out with a pad of paper and a pen. "Any of you ever write a song before?" he asked.

"I've tried writing lyrics," I said. The operative word here was "tried."

What came first, melody or words? We didn't have a clue. Where exactly did songs come from? Were they carefully thought out, or did they just drop out of the sky? My guess was that it was a combination. Sometimes they came out of nowhere—sometimes it was just a hell of a lot of tinkering until you got it right. And what made a great song? Was it great words? Probably not. Just like you could have a goofy-sounding band name, you could have pretty goofy words. A great guitar riff covered a multitude of sins.

A song just plain had to sound good, we decided. Lyrics were not the problem. We needed a great sound. And that put the burden on me. I couldn't name a single band whose sound was distinct because of the bass player or drummer. It was guitar playing that mattered—that and vocals.

We fiddled around all afternoon, coming up with various song beginnings, interesting riffs, and words to go along with them. Nothing was clicking, but we had fun trying. After a while, Tuck disappeared inside again and came back with an iPod that he hooked up to a portable player. We played classic song after classic song. Once again, I realized there was no rhyme or reason as to why something worked. It just plain sounded good.

Before we knew it, three hours had gone by. "Same time tomorrow?" I asked.

Tuck nodded, and Vern and I piled into the Trap and headed for home.

"I loved that," Vern said as we started up Casitas Pass. "We sounded like shit, but I loved trying to make something happen."

"Yeah," I said. I knew what he meant. I couldn't quite put it into words. We were building something, and we had no idea where we were going with it, or where it would take us. What kind of sound? We didn't know, and that was the fun of it.

The three hours I spent trying to come up with songs with the band inspired me. After Vern dropped me off, I got out a piece of paper and kept experimenting with song lyrics. I thought back over our common experiences of the last few months. Time spent with Vern and Tuck. Hours in the Trap.

Suddenly I was writing. I had no tune in mind, but I liked the words that were coming out.

TEMPLIN HIGHWAY

It's raining outside and we're in the Trap
A cold can of chili in my lap
You ask me to pull your finger but I ain't bitin'
'Cuz when you let it rip, soon we'll be fightin'
Letting 'em go at point-blank range
Ain't this song kinda strange?

Damn. I thought I was onto something. I started on another song. It was called "I Know Your Knees Want Me—How About the Rest of You?" Then I wrote one called "Hey, Jerry, You're Big and Hairy." I was on a songwriting roll. I wrote a song called "Kiss Me Quick Before the Porch Light Comes On," then one called "The Old Man Across the Street Thinks We're Funny."

Write what you know, I'd always heard. And it was working.

Mom came home in the middle of my songwriting. "What are you up to, Elroy?" she asked. She picked up a sheet of paper off the floor. " 'Hey, Jerry, You're Big and Hairy'?"

"They're songs, Mom. I'm starting a band with Vern and Tuck."

"Really?" She read the lyrics to the song. I was so glad I hadn't written anything about jumping bones. Then she grabbed another sheet and read it. Then another. She looked up at me. "Really?"

"It will sound better when I put it to music. Add a hot melody and some great guitar, you'll see."

She just stood there going through my song lyrics. I couldn't read her facial expression. Did she like them? Did she not? She wouldn't say. I kept writing while she went over to the kitchen and started cooking dinner, which smelled like macaroni and cheese.

After dinner she got up from the table. "I have to go out for a few hours."

"It's dark out, Mom." My mother never went anywhere at night. Once she was home, she was home for good.

"I won't be long. You'll do the dishes, won't you, Elroy?"

I pointed to the window. "It's dark out. Bad guys, Mom. Monsters." But she was already grabbing her jacket. "Where are you going?"

"I won't be gone long." She checked her face in the mirror by the door and was gone.

Before I started on the dishes, I wrote another song: "Gotta Get Home Before the Monsters Come Out." Then I wrote one called "Late-Night Rendezvous." If she had a boyfriend, I was going to shoot myself.

CHAPTER TWENTY-THREE

The band was coming along. I decided to make "Templin Highway" into a regular road song, no farting references. It was all about getting out of Dodge, or Highmont Ridge, for that matter. But it was very California. Vern and Tuck put in their two cents about heading to the Eastern Sierra, about certain highways we'd been on. Guess it made sense. I couldn't see a farting song gaining wide acceptance, even with a really great guitar riff.

Our strong points seemed to be guitar and drums, although Vern was getting better on bass. He stepped up his lessons to three days a week. We'd be ready for Battle of the Bands.

"You're not going for the torn-jeans, ripped-T-shirt look, are you?" Juana Maria put a finger down her throat and fake-gagged. "It's so overdone. Be original, Elroy."

"What would you call original?"

Juana Maria and I had worked the lunch shift together.

Now we were off and walking through the mall. I felt a little weird wearing my puffy work shirt, but she was in her peasant-girl outfit—if she could handle the stares, so could I.

Turns out, no one was staring.

"You know what I think is sexy?" she asked.

"Scarlett Johansson?"

She elbowed me. "I mean, you know what I think is sexy on a *guy*?"

"What?"

"A bow tie."

"Thank God you didn't say a G-string." She elbowed me again. "Seriously, Juana Maria, a rock band wearing bow ties would be ridiculous, don't you think?"

She stopped and looked at me. Really looked at me, from top to bottom. "Pretend like you're holding a guitar." I struck my best rock-star pose. "Now strum." I did, while she stared at my Adam's apple. "Yeah, I guess that would be a little weird. No bow tie, but don't go for the grunge look, either."

I stopped strumming my imaginary guitar. People were beginning to look at me funny. "So what do you suggest?" I asked her.

We were standing before the entrance to Macy's. She pulled me inside. "Come with me." She led me through the store to the men's department and started going through a rack of dress shirts. "Okay, my second choice. Know what else I think looks great?"

"Beyoncé?"

This time she punched me in the arm. "I mean on a guy."

I shrugged.

"Blue jeans and a dress shirt. You can still rock and you won't look like you're a homeless dork."

"I'd hate to look like a dork," I told her.

She pulled a blue dress shirt off the rack and held it up to me. "Here, try this on."

"What?"

"The dressing room's over there." She pointed behind me. "Go try it on. I'll keep looking."

I took it and went into the dressing room. While I was buttoning it up, another shirt hit me in the face. "Here's another one," she called. "I'll be waiting out here."

I checked myself out in the mirror, then opened the door to let her see. She walked up and did some tugging, checking the fit. "Oh, I'm good. This is it. This is the look for—" She stopped. "What was the name of your band again?"

"Templin Highway."

"Yes, Templin Highway. Wear jeans and dress shirts, Elroy. You look hot!"

It was the first time a member of the opposite sex had said I looked hot. She wasn't so bad herself, standing there before me, flashing her dimples. "Uh . . . can you say that again?"

"You look hot!"

I blushed—big-time.

"You're not too bad yourself," I told her. Which was a major understatement. If only she had a normal father. Getting your knees bashed by a baseball bat had to hurt. Ernesto had made it clear that Juana Maria was off limits. Damn shame.

"Thanks," she said.

During band practice, I introduced the idea of dress shirts to Vern and Tuck. "Dress shirts?" Vern said.

"Dress shirts?" Tuck repeated. "Who wears dress shirts? I thought we could go bare-chested and wear war paint."

I thought this over. After all, I did have pecs. I shook my head. "Nah." And Vern looked relieved. He was practically pecless. "We're not a metal band. We need to wear shirts. I have it on good authority that jeans and dress shirts are sexy."

"Sexy is good," Vern said. He turned to Tuck for confirmation.

"Sexy *is* good," Tuck said. "But who's your good authority? Say your grandma and you die."

"A girl I know," I said. "She's our age. I trust her taste."

"I'll think on it," Tuck said.

"Me too. But sexy is good, Tuck." Vern and I were on the same page. Rock and roll was a means to an end. And if a girl our age said something was sexy, we'd better pay attention.

I plugged the guitar into the amp, and we started in on our lead song, "Templin Highway." Vern was getting pretty good on bass. As a test, I sped up the song, and he stayed with me, anticipating each chord change.

"Guys!" Tuck yelled. "Stay with your drummer. Hear that?" He stepped on the foot pedal a few times. "That's what you call the beat. We need to be together on this."

"I know." I pointed my pick at Vern. "Just testing our bass player here. One more time. Two, three, four . . ."

We started in again on "Templin Highway." I couldn't wait to do it before an audience.

There was no longer an empty rectangle on my dad's whiteboard. It had more detail. I squirted some maple syrup onto my pancakes and pointed. "One of your mental irons in the fire?"

"Kind of," he said. "The beginning stages of something. Actually, way more than the beginning stages, but we'll see."

The rectangle had a line drawn down the middle, dividing it into two sections. Obviously, some kind of crude architect's drawing. In one of the boxes it said "Shop." The other side was left blank. It also showed entrances, exits, windows, and a bathroom.

"Shop?" I asked.

He nodded.

"What's the other area for?"

Dad swallowed and took a sip of coffee. "I'll tell you later."

How vague. "You know, Dad, Mom's not real big on you being an entrepreneur."

"I know that," he said. I could tell he didn't want to discuss it further. In fact, he got up from the table and wiped off the whiteboard.

"You didn't have to do that," I told him. When he sat back down, I decided to change the subject. "We're thinking of wearing jeans and dress shirts for Battle of the Bands. What do you think?"

"The Beatles wore suits."

"Suits?"

"Yep, jackets and ties."

Tuck was having a hard time swallowing the idea of dress shirts. I knew he wouldn't go for jackets and ties. "I can't see wearing a suit and trying to rock," I said.

"The Beatles rocked in suits."

I grabbed the plates and took them to the sink. "Maybe I'll wait until my first gold album."

"If you get a gold album, *I'll* pay for the suit."

"Sounds like a plan," I said.

I started winning in wrestling, and in a roundabout way I had Carol Ann to thank for it. It began the Monday after the backwards dance. Maybe replaying the Elroy Gets Rejected tape over and over in my head did something. At practice that day, I took Mike Thomas down. Not in some kind of forced cartwheel move; I just double-legged him. Then I let him up and did it again. When he went down a third time, everyone in the room was watching, as if some third-grader had just slam-dunked over LeBron James.

Coach Grogan pulled me aside after practice. "What's gotten into you, Elroy?"

"Exactly," Mike said.

Getting rejected by two girls had gotten into me. Being threatened by a big, hairy, ugly guy had gotten into me. The Second Base Club in general had gotten into me. And it just happened to come out at practice that day.

It was perfect timing, because our league tournament was coming up. Maybe getting dumped would keep me focused, make me hungry to win.

CHAPTER TWENTY-FOUR

The number-two man in the Second Base Club had it in for me. I knew that. If I ever found myself alone with him, he'd kick my ass. Of course, I was never alone. I made sure of it. But Sampson Teague was another matter. He was nothing like Hairy Jerry. He was never anything but friendly toward me.

We were at weight-training class, working our way around the universal gym. Shoulder press, bench press, lats, triceps.

"How's the band coming along?" he asked after a while.

"Not too bad." I told him about Battle of the Bands. "If you're not doing anything on April 7, come on by the fairgrounds. I'd like an honest opinion: Do we rock or do we not?"

He said he would. We were both sweating now as we kept working through our circuit.

"So, Sampson," I said, "you're not with Marisa anymore?" It was the question I'd been dying to ask ever since seeing him with a different girl at the backwards dance.

He was in mid-curl and stopped. "Marisa Caldwell?" He let the weights fall.

"Yeah."

He shook his head and began curling again. "No. Nice girl, but no. I'm more of a love-'em-and-leave-'em type. Variety is the spice of life. Isn't that right, Elroy?"

I wasn't sure, although I'd heard that was the case.

"You know Marisa?" Sampson asked.

"Kind of. Almost had something going with her, once upon a time. Haven't talked to her in a while, but I used to see you two together. Now I don't. Just wondered what happened."

He put down the dumbbells, and I grabbed some and started curling. Sampson gave me a weird look.

"What's wrong?" I asked.

"Just kind of surprised, I guess," he said. "You and Marisa Caldwell? Nice going."

"I said I *almost* had something going with her."

"Still," he said, "Marisa Caldwell. You aim high, Elroy. I'm impressed."

"Thanks." I finished my set of curls, and we moved on to the leg press.

That afternoon, Vern and I met up at Tuck's for band practice. We worked out the kinks in our signature song. Vern was getting better on bass, Tuck and I were pretty tight on guitar and drums, and vocals were coming along. We planned on surprising a few people when we got onstage to perform it in front of an audience.

Once we got "Templin Highway" to where we could do it forward and backward, with our eyes closed, standing on our heads, we went on to a few backup numbers. We played until someone complained of sore fingers or arms. This was usually Vern, since he had the least experience.

"No more! Uncle!" Vern said finally, showing me his dented fingertips.

"You need to build up some calluses," I told him.

"Believe me, I'm getting there." He waggled his fingers. "You could strike a match on these babies."

I looked at Tuck, who was rotating his shoulders from two hours of drumming. "See you guys tomorrow," he said. "We sounded good today."

Chapter Twenty-Five

Hairy Jerry was giving me some pretty serious death stares from across the quad. I knew about the Second Base Club, and he knew I knew. I watched my back like never before. If I had to pee I used the bathroom in the administration building—didn't want to get jumped—and I never went alone. Vern or Tuck, usually both of them, were always with me.

I finished wrestling season with an 8–8 record. Most of my wins came the second half of the season. I called it my post–Carol Ann victory streak. And at our JV league tournament I placed third. Not bad for a first-year wrestler. Mom and Dad were there to see me step on the block to receive my medal.

Even though I joined for all the wrong reasons (reason), I have to admit that I loved being on a team. I didn't love it as much as I loved making music with Vern and Tuck, but I loved competing. I loved working hard at something. And seeing Mom and Dad together so much gave me all kinds of hope. They were together because of me. How could that be bad?

We went out to dinner to celebrate my fairly successful wrestling season. The three of us. Mom and Dad sat across from me in a booth over at Mickey Moose.

Dad held up a glass of iced tea. "To Elroy," he said.

I clinked glasses with him. So did Mom.

"Thanks," I said. "I survived."

"You did way more than survive," Mom said. "You medaled."

"Thanks," I said again. "By the way, you two look good to-gether."

"Well, she looks good anyway," Dad said.

And Mom gave me her don't-get-your-hopes-up look.

I couldn't help it. They *did* look good together. My hopes were way up.

There were two weeks left before the band competition at the fairgrounds. We practiced every day, long hours, ignoring Vern's complaints about sore fingers, letting our schoolwork slip. We had bigger goals than getting good grades. We wanted to woo women. At least, Vern and I did.

When April 7 came around, we were ready. I was able to talk Vern into wearing a dress shirt, but not Tuck. He said he planned to break a sweat and would be wearing a tank top. I was fine with that. He'd be hidden behind the drums. Vern and I would be out front.

"Leave the John Deere cap at home, Tuck," I told him. "This is rock and roll, not *Hee Haw*."

"Yes, master."

"This may have been a mistake, guys," I said. We were back-stage at Battle of the Bands. The fairgrounds stadium was packed.

"No one is doing original songs. We're going to get booed off the stage."

"It'll be fine," Tuck said. "Just start in on 'Templin Highway' like we practiced. Don't hold back. If they love us, we'll go to the next song."

I nodded. Sticking to the game plan seemed like a good idea. We were twelfth in a lineup of about fifteen bands. And every one of them that had gone on so far had absolutely rocked, except one. A band called Spastic Pajamas. Oddly enough, their front man wore a bow tie. They didn't get booed off the stage, but the applause was pretty sporadic. And someone threw a tomato. Tough crowd.

Vern slung his bass over his shoulder and looked like he was about ready to throw up. "Two bands to go."

Butterflies banged around inside me. Tuck twirled his drumsticks and pointed one of them at me. "Strong vocals, Elroy. If you're tentative, we're sunk."

"Got it." The crowd erupted in applause as the band onstage started in on an Aerosmith song. This was not Battle of the Bands; it was Battle of Who Could Cover Someone Else's Song the Best. The Aerosmith song ended, and the band left the stage.

"Ladies and gentlemen, please welcome Pie Fight."

"We're up next," Vern said. He was almost shaking. So was I.

"Fire up," Tuck said. He grabbed the Skoal can from his back pocket and offered us a mint. Vern and I took two each.

Pie Fight played three cover songs and did a pretty good job of it. They'd be a tough act to follow.

"Ladies and gentlemen, please welcome our next band, Templin Highway."

"That's us," Tuck said, holding out a fist to me. I smacked it with my own. "Remember, don't hold back, Elroy. They'll dig us if we're confident."

"I'm ready," I told him. We climbed the stairs onto the stage and plugged in the guitar and bass. The amps and drums were provided, which made it easier to transition from band to band. Tuck banged his sticks together, tapping out the beat, and I went to the microphone. I looked out on the crowd and saw a familiar face. Sampson Teague was in the third row, along with a few of his Second Base Club cronies. No sign of Hairy Jerry.

"Good evening," I said into the mike, "we're Templin Highway," which was kind of lame, since we'd already been introduced. Then I hit the first chord hard. A second later, Vern came in on bass, and Tuck was right there with us on percussion. So far so good. The intro was fairly long. I could see the faces in the crowd wondering, *Is this a new version of a classic? Are they eventually going to hit that familiar melody?* I knew what they were expecting. Too bad. I was sorry to disappoint, but not too sorry.

I began to sing:

Driving down the highway, Springsteen soundin' good
Never comin' back, don't think I should

The facial expressions in the crowd began to change. People turned to one another. *This isn't a familiar classic. These guys have the gall to play something original.*

It was the only game plan we had, and I was sticking to it. We played on as the audience began to fidget and look around.

Never comin' back, I say. Never comin' back

Halfway through the song, someone yelled, "Get off the stage!"

Vern and I exchanged a look, but we kept playing. Tuck kept going on drums.

Things never spoken, things never said
Wondering if it's too late now—

Something whizzed by my head. Couldn't tell what it was until a few seconds later, when something squishy and wet glanced off my guitar. A tomato, an overripe tomato.

"Get off the stage!"

Another projectile whizzed by. I didn't stop singing. Nor did my band-mates stop playing. Instead, I changed the lyrics.

I'm quitting my job, quitting work
Whoever threw that tomato is the world's biggest jerk

I scanned the audience and found the perp, who was winding up for another throw. I pointed to him and kept chanting the melody of the song, with the new lyrics:

You jerk, you jerk, you jeee-eeerk

I sidestepped his next throw and sang it again.

You jerk, you jerk, you assho-o-ole

Then I turned around, unplugged the guitar, and walked off the stage. Vern followed my lead. Tuck snapped his sticks over his thigh and chucked them into the crowd.

At the bottom of the stage stairs, Sampson Teague was standing there waiting for me. "Strange audience, Elroy. They just wanted to hear something familiar."

I ran a hand through my hair, pulled out a glob of rotten tomato, and flung it to the ground. "Yeah, whatever." I turned to go around him when I heard—

"Elroy!" It was Juana Maria.

"Hey," I said.

"That guy was a jerk. But . . . uh . . . you kind of rocked!" She pointed to my blue dress shirt. "And you look great."

"I gotta go," I told her. I'd just played in my first-ever rock concert and been hit by a vegetable for my efforts. I didn't want to stay and chat. Not with Juana Maria, not with anyone. "I'll see you later. I gotta go."

The announcer was introducing the next group, a band called Bicycle Pump. Sampson and Juana Maria were still standing there, looking at me like they had more to say. I wasn't in the mood to listen. "I have to go," I told them.

Vern got the car, and we piled in.

"Shit!" I banged my head on the dashboard. Vern put a hand on my shoulder, but I shook it off. "Get me out of this place," I said.

"Can you be a little more specific?"

"Take me home."

We drove through the dark streets of Highmont Ridge. Tuck said, "Whose idea was it to start a rock band?" I could hear him cracking his knuckles, getting ready to inflict pain. "Was it yours, Elroy?"

"It was Vern's," I said.

Tuck cocked his fist like he was going to punch him. Instead, he patted him on the back. "It was a good idea, Vern. There are jerks out there. It was still a good idea."

Vern shook his head. "That guy wasn't a jerk." He turned to me. "Tell him, Elroy."

I didn't feel like telling anything to anyone.

"Tell him, Elroy."

"Tell him what? That he wasn't a jerk?"

"Yes. He was an . . ." He gestured for me to finish.

"He was an assho-o-ole," Tuck sang from the back seat. "You were awesome, though, Elroy. Got hit by a tomato and kept singing. Amazing."

I didn't feel amazing, or awesome. "Just take me home," I said. "I'm going to take a shower and forget this whole thing." That was the plan, anyway. But I knew no amount of soap and water would do the job. We'd just spent months creating what we thought was the perfect song. And they hated us.

"Forget this whole thing?" Tuck said. "You mean forget about being tomatoed, or forget that we're in a rock-and-roll band? Am I the only one who wants to keep playing music?"

We didn't answer right away.

Then Vern said, "I'm still in."

He pulled to a stop in front of the Airstream, and I got out and grabbed my guitar. Tuck jumped into the front seat. "I'll think about it," I said. But I really didn't want to think about anything. I wanted to go inside and shut the door and not think at all.

Tuck said, "We rocked, Elroy. We really did. We just have to find our venue." He waved. "Take a shower. You have tomato on you. And remember . . ."

I turned. "Yes?"

"He was an assho-o-ole," he sang as Vern stepped on the gas.

CHAPTER TWENTY-SIX

It was the longest shower in history. After I got all the dried tomato off my face, I stayed under the hot stream of water and thought it over. How badly did I want to play in a rock-and-roll band? I couldn't decide. All I knew was that a hot shower was a pretty fabulous thing. That is, until Mom started banging on the door, reminding me that we were on a septic tank and she didn't want to have the thing pumped.

I got dressed and went into the living room and flopped on the couch, letting out a huge sigh. Mixed with a groan.

Mom wasn't drilling me with the eyeball stare. In its place was something resembling compassion.

"They hated us, Mom," I said.

"What happened?"

I told her about the concert and she listened the way moms are supposed to listen, with all necessary "ooh"s and "ah"s and "that's too bads." It felt good to get it all out, and to have a sympathetic ear listening.

"Vern and Tuck want to keep playing music," I said.

"And you don't?"

"I'm not sure."

Mom nodded, the compassionate look still on her face. "Let me ask you something, Elroy. How did you feel about the band before you got onstage, when it was just you, Vern, and Tuck trying to come up with something?"

I knew where she was going with this, that it's not always about the end product, it's about the process. Only I didn't want to hear it right now.

"Who cares?" I grumbled.

"You do. You're just not willing to admit it. Yet."

Yet. That was the operative word. I'd told Vern and Tuck I'd think about it, and I would. Just not now.

My phone vibrated and I grabbed it. A text from Vern.

road trip eastern sierra.
picking up tuck
will come get u.

I looked at the phone in my hand. I'd been so focused on Battle of the Bands that I'd forgotten about our spring break trip.

"What is it?" Mom asked.

"Vern. Coming by to get me. Remember I told you about going camping in the Eastern Sierra?"

"Not really." She crossed her arms. She was no longer in ooh-and-aah mode.

"We never celebrated Vern's new car properly. It's kind of a combination road trip/camping trip."

"He's coming over now?" She pointed out the window. "It's the middle of the night."

"Best time to drive through the desert."

The more I talked about it, the more I realized that I needed this trip. After all that had happened at the fairgrounds, getting out of town for a few days would be perfect.

But Mom didn't look happy.

"Is it okay if I go?" I asked.

"It's the middle of the night!" she said again.

A few minutes later, we heard the Trap rumbling up Casitas Pass. Mom opened the door, and Vern and Tuck stepped inside.

"Trust me," Vern said. "You don't want to drive through the Mojave Desert during the daytime with no air conditioning." This was his explanation for leaving at night.

Mom said she wouldn't want to drive anywhere, at any time, in Vern's machine. She couldn't bring herself to call it a car. It was just some kind of thing that made a lot of noise. It had four wheels and an engine, but it didn't qualify as an automobile. I could see her point. But the Trap got us places, and it didn't break down. Yet.

I turned to Tuck. "Did you bring the tent poles this time?"

"Hell, yes." He shot my mom a look. "Make that 'Heck, yes.'"

I'd never told my mom about Templin Highway and the Night of Gas. It was our private memory, and one that I was trying hard to forget. "What about food, lantern, stove?"

"We'll get food in Bishop. We have the rest."

"So all you need is my sweet presence? Is that what you're saying?"

Vern and Tuck looked at each other but said nothing. I went to the hall closet and pulled down my sleeping bag and duffle, tossed in some clothes, and zipped it up.

Mom didn't exactly say I could go. Then again, she didn't

say I couldn't, and that was good enough for me. A nonnegative was a positive. I really needed this, and maybe she understood.

To my surprise, Tuck took the back seat. I was ready to fight for the front, but he climbed into the back with no argument.

"To the man who took a tomato in the face and kept on singing. Elroy, I award you shotgun for the duration of the trip."

Actually, I took a tomato on my guitar. The splatter is what hit my face.

I stood there looking at the front seat as if it had been booby-trapped. And I was no booby. I ran my hand over the seat just to be sure it wasn't rigged.

"Have a seat, Elroy. You're the man."

I climbed in, and Vern fired up the car and we pulled away from the Airstream. Mom was standing in the doorway with her fingers in her ears, shaking her head. I smiled and waved. The Trap might be a piece of crap, but it was *our* piece of crap.

"The Eastern Sierra or bust," Vern yelled.

"Let's not talk about girls right now," I said.

Vern looked at me. "Excuse me?"

"You said 'bust.' I just thought this trip should be all about us. A real guy trip, you know?"

"I didn't say 'Eastern Sierra or breast.' I said 'bust.' "

"Exactly." We all laughed. It felt good to be on the road. I couldn't explain it, but there was something about leaving Highmont Ridge that had me excited. I didn't want to think about Templin Highway (the band) or the incident at the fairgrounds. I just wanted to get out of town and hang with the boys.

We took the 126 east, and Vern turned on the stereo and cranked it way up so we could hear it over the considerable roar of the engine.

"You really need to get that muffler," I yelled.

"One of these days."

We drove on, shooting past Santa Paula and Fillmore. No one spoke for maybe an hour. Vern turned onto the 5 south, and then the 14 north, toward Mojave.

After a while, I turned down the music. "I never answered your question, Tuck," I said.

"What question was that again?"

"If you're the only ones who want to keep making music. The answer is no, you and Vern are not the only ones. I'm still in. No cover songs, though. Original songs only."

"Or bust?" Vern asked.

"Or bust," I told him.

Vern held up a palm and I slapped it. Then I turned around and banged fists with Tuck.

"But right now I think sleeping is in order." I checked that the passenger door was locked and leaned my head against it.

"I concur," Tuck said, flopping down in the back. "You got the wheel, Vern?"

"I do. You guys sleep tight. I'll wake you if I get tired."

I fell into some sort of half-sleep, where the music and the sound of the engine melded into my dreams. At some level I knew I was in the Trap, but, then again, I didn't. Hours clicked by . . . or maybe it was just minutes. In my head I kept getting tomatoed while playing the music coming from Vern's stereo.

Then, suddenly, my eyes were wide open. Vern was yelling, "Oh my God! Oh my God!"

I sat up, blinking at the highway in front of me. "What is it?"

Tuck popped up in the back seat. "What's the matter?"

"I don't know if I should tell you."

"What is it?" I said again.

"Tell us, Vern," Tuck said.

"I just woke up," Vern said.

There was a pause as Tuck and I took this in; then Tuck said, "Pull over, Vern."

"I'm fine, really. It was only a little catnap."

"A little catnap at sixty-five miles an hour?"

Vern looked at me and nodded. "The man does have a point." He pulled to the side of the highway and got out. I grabbed my cell phone and checked the time—two-forty-six. We were still twenty minutes away from Mojave.

"Coffee break at the next stop," I said. "If you want to drive, Tuck, I'll stay up with you."

"I'm okay now," Vern said. "I can drive. Really."

"No!" Tuck and I said together.

And so, technically, I didn't get shotgun for the duration of the trip. It was a combination of driver's seat and shotgun. Vern would get another chance to drive later, when the sun was up and shining. Meanwhile, Tuck and I took over in two-hour shifts.

After stopping in Mojave for gas and coffee, we hit a long stretch of highway that went on and on. Somewhere to our left, the mountains began to rise as we headed north. While Tuck drove, I got out a map and clicked on the overhead light. "Where exactly are we going?" I asked.

"Eastern Sierra," Tuck said.

"I know, but where? The Eastern Sierra is a pretty big place." The Sierras ran for hundreds of miles. Anywhere from Lone Pine to Lake Tahoe would qualify as the eastern side. I looked up and saw Tuck leaning toward me, staring at the map. "Eyes on the road, big guy."

I folded up the map and put it away so as not to tempt the driver. Vern had already taken a nap while at the wheel. I didn't want to die.

"Mammoth," Tuck said finally. "Some of the best fishing in the western United States."

I nodded. "Sounds good." I turned up the stereo to drown out Vern's snoring, and we drove on. Two hours later, we stopped in Lone Pine for a combination pee-and-switch-drivers break. Vern didn't wake up. I grabbed a soda to keep the caffeine surging, then got behind the wheel, and we drove on. Tuck sat in the passenger seat and stayed up to make sure I did. We shot past the small towns of Independence and Big Pine. The sky was turning from black to gray. Sometime later, I realized I didn't need headlights anymore. I also noticed Vern was sitting up in the back seat, the contours of my duffle embedded in his face.

"You're an attractive man, Vern Zuckman."

"Where are we?"

"Five minutes south of Bishop."

We got supplies in Bishop, population four thousand and about the same elevation. Then the highway began to climb as we shot past Rock Creek, Crowley Lake, and Convict, the terrain changing from high-desert cactus to pine trees and log cabins. An hour later, we were cruising the streets of Mammoth Lakes. The elevation had doubled, and patches of snow lined the road. I was pretty sure Vern would wake up with a snowball in his sleeping bag before the trip was over, payback for falling asleep at the wheel.

We drove up to the ski slopes, where it was still open for business, then down the back side of the mountain, Tuck pointing the way.

"Where are we going?" Vern asked.

"San Joaquin River, best fishing in the Eastern Sierra." Tuck reached into the back seat and grabbed his fly reel and began fiddling with it. "First one who catches a fish wins."

"You're on," I said. I didn't know what the prize would be, but I was up for the challenge.

Chapter Twenty-Seven

The thing about camping is that there's no sleeping in. The sun makes itself known pretty darn early—so do the birds— and in the High Sierra in early April you freeze your ass off all night long, and the only thing on your mind is getting up and starting a fire as quickly as possible.

We were camped at a place called Soda Springs, along the San Joaquin River, and I'd just survived the coldest night of my life. I had on every piece of clothing I'd brought, my sleeping bag zipped tight around me, and I was still freezing. I couldn't move my toes. We'd spent the previous day getting skunked on the river, fol- lowed by a night of freezing. Whose idea was it to go camping?

On the flip side, no one had gas. Yet.

I stumbled out of the tent and saw Tuck pouring gasoline over a pile of wood in the fire ring.

"Isn't that cheating?"

"You want Jeremiah Johnson, or do you want warmth?"

"Warmth sounds good."

"Stand back." He struck a match and dropped it.

Whooosh!

Flames shot up over our heads for a few seconds, then settled down to a normal campfire, popping and crackling. Tuck and I moved closer. The tent unzipped behind us, and Vern poked his head out. "I heard a whoosh," he said. Just like me, he was wearing every piece of clothing he'd brought. He joined us at the fire. "Froze my ass off last night."

"Join the party," I told him.

"I'm trying to. Move over."

I roasted both sides of myself until I had to remove my extra layers. My friends did the same. Two hours later, the sun crept into the campground, and I began to feel I could move about like a normal person.

Tuck said we'd been skunked on the river the day before because of the full moon—the fish had been feeding all night. Today should be better. They'd be in the mood to eat.

I hoped so. I could endure a freezing night or two if something worthwhile happened during the day, like catching a load of fish. After breakfast, we grabbed our rods and headed to the river. Vern and I used salmon eggs with a few split-shot weights to keep them below the surface. Tuck had his fly rod. He wouldn't stoop to using bait.

We fished all morning, wandering up and down the San Joaquin. At some point I lost track of Vern. Tuck was still in sight. He wandered over to me after a while.

"Hey," he said, "you know what?"

"No, but I know his brother Who."

He shook away my attempt at a joke. "One of my girlfriends has a friend coming in from out of state. Nice-looking girl. And she's going to need a date."

One of his girl*friends*? "I'm sorry. What did you say?" I couldn't get past the idea of multiple girlfriends.

Tuck repeated himself. Then he added, "You want to double-date?"

"So she's fat and ugly. Is that what you're saying?"

Tuck flicked his fly out onto the water and let it drift below a rock, never taking his eye off it. "Nope. I saw a photo. She looks hot."

"Why me?" I asked. "Why not Vern?"

Tuck glanced up and down the river. "You're here. Vern's not. You want me to ask him instead?"

"No. I'm interested. But if she weighs three hundred pounds, you die."

"Fair enough. I'll set it up for next weekend."

A girl from another state. Who knows, maybe bagging a California boy was what she had in mind. I moved downriver to a place where the fast water flowed into a deep pool. But the fish weren't interested. I wandered back up to Tuck and said, "You know what?"

"No, but I know his brother Who." He grinned.

"The fish aren't biting. I could go for a nap."

Tuck nodded and reeled in his line. "A nap sounds good. I didn't sleep at all last night."

"Yeah, freezing your ass off will do that."

Back at camp, we found patches of sunlight and spread out our sleeping bags in them. I was asleep almost immediately. I dreamed of rock-and-roll music again—and tomatoes. Only they didn't smell like tomatoes. It was more like rotting fish. Vern was on bass and kept saying my name over and over again. "Elroy, Elroy, Elroy."

I opened my eyes and came face to face with an eighteen-inch rainbow trout. Vern was waving it under my nose. "Elroy, Elroy, Elroy."

I sat up. "How'd you guys do?"

"Skunked," I said.

"Skunked," repeated Tuck.

"So I win. Lay the prize on me."

Tuck walked over and gave him a hug.

"No, really," Vern said. "I want the prize."

"That was the prize," Tuck said. "Women would pay good money for that."

"You suck, Mayfield."

The next morning, we packed up and drove out of the San Joaquin River Valley to Mammoth Lakes. It was only our third day, but we all looked like we'd been sleeping in the dirt for weeks, and we smelled of smoke.

"There's gotta be a place around here to shower," Tuck said.

That was the plan. Find a place where we could get cleaned up before starting the seven-hour drive back to Highmont. We stopped at a ski shop in Mammoth to ask about a shower but came away empty—they didn't know. We got back into the car and were moving on when Vern suddenly began yelling, "Gas station, gas station, pull over."

I checked the gas gauge. "We're fine on gas, Vern. We'll fill up in Lone Pine."

"No. I need to use the facilities!"

I looked at his face and saw how he was clutching his stomach. This was no laughing matter. It could be way worse than Templin Highway and the Night of Gas if I didn't find a gas station, and quick. I pulled over at a Shell station, and Vern jumped out and sprinted to the men's room. Actually, it was more of a sprint/walk—pretty hard to go fast when you're squeezing your cheeks together.

Before he got back, Tuck was doubled over in pain. "Must have been the Vern Zuckman Surprise," he said.

Vern Zuckman Surprise was our dinner the night before. It was Vern's trout mixed with rice, chili, spaghetti noodles, and just a hint of pinecone. It wasn't bad-tasting, but obviously it wreaked havoc with the human digestive system.

Tuck got out of the car and headed for the bathroom, cheeks flexing the whole way. "Vern, hurry it up."

It was a good twenty minutes before I saw Vern and Tuck again. When I did, they were smiling. And they'd found a place where we could shower. "There's a boarding house down the street," Vern said. "Showers for three bucks."

They directed me to the boarding house, a place called Miss Watson's, and we went in. The girl at the desk was an older version of Marisa, which is to say hot and then some. Vern and I looked to Tuck to do the talking, since we were in the presence of beauty and had temporarily lost our ability to speak.

Tuck shook his head at us in disgust, then said, "We'd like to take showers."

"Yes," the girl said, smiling, "I was just going to recommend that." She fanned the air in front of her face. "Seriously."

She gave us towels and directed us down the hall. "Soap and shampoo are provided."

I went first. The hallway door opened directly into a tiny changing area about two feet square, which was right next to a glass shower door. I stripped and turned on the water as hot as I could take it. Soon I had soap all over me, well on my way to becoming civilized again . . . and that's when the Vern Zuckman Surprise hit. It was the Templin Highway and the Night of Gas all over again, only this time it wanted out of my body in solid form. Or liquid form. I wasn't exactly sure.

I burst out of the shower stall and into the hallway, water pouring off me, every inch of my body covered with suds. "Where's the bathroom?!"

Vern and Tuck, who were sitting in chairs reading newspapers, looked at me, not really registering that there was a naked Elroy in front of them, covered in soap, holding his privates.

"I need a bathroom!"

They saw the desperation in my eyes and burst out laughing. The commotion brought the Marisa-caliber receptionist into the hallway. Her hands flew to her gaping mouth.

"Bathroom!" I yelled, no longer able to communicate in full sentences.

She took two steps toward me and opened a door. I sprinted to her—she didn't bother to avert her eyes—got inside and shut the door behind me. By the time I emerged, everything had dried, but there was no longer panic on my face. I strolled back to the shower.

"See you guys in a few minutes," I told my friends. They were no longer laughing, but I could hear them start up again as soon as I closed the door.

Later, as we were heading down the mountain toward Bishop with Vern at the wheel, Tuck tapped me on the shoulder.

"So, Elroy, I need to ask you a question, and I want you to be honest."

"Shoot."

"Is that the first time you've been naked in the presence of the opposite sex?"

"Yes," I told him. "But don't tell my mom."

CHAPTER TWENTY-EIGHT

We stopped for gas in Lone Pine. Vern pumped while Tuck and I headed into the store for supplies. On the way back to the car, Tuck stopped me.

"We need to talk," he said.

"About?"

"The blind date."

"The blind date with Shamu?"

"You need to come prepared."

"With a harpoon?" I looked over at the Trap, where Vern was busy cleaning the windshield.

"I'm serious," Tuck said. "Do I have to spell it out for you?"

"I wish you would." Vern had finished the windshield and was looking at us with his best what's-up expression.

"Condoms," Tuck said.

"I thought you were going to spell it out for me."

"Fine. C-o-n-d-o-m-s." He slapped me on the back and headed toward to the car. "Just in case. Elroy might get lucky."

I just might. But I had to admit the thought scared me. I'd kissed a couple of times, but that was it. What if she wanted more? What if she really wanted to bag a California boy and I didn't know what to do? The thought had me terrified and excited at the same time.

As soon as we got back to Highmont Ridge, I headed to the Walgreens. I wandered the aisles, not able to bring myself to ask where they kept the condoms. The assistant manager, who was a lady about my mom's age, kept watching me like I was some kind of criminal.

"Can I help you, young man?" she asked finally. She had on reading glasses connected to a chain around her neck and was looking at me over the tops of the lenses.

"Uh . . . help me? Why would I need help?"

"Because you've been wandering the same aisle for fifteen minutes now."

I'd found the condom aisle. I just couldn't bring myself to grab one of the boxes. And I certainly wasn't going to do so with Miss Reading Glasses watching.

She cleared her throat.

"Uh . . . where do you keep the Gatorade?"

"I see," she said. "You're looking for Gatorade in this section."

"I'm new in town?" It came out like a question. "It's hot out and I'm thirsty?" I could feel myself starting to sweat. A cool drink would come in handy, come to think of it.

The lady pointed to the far wall, where the word DRINKS hung in gigantic letters. It was the largest sign in the store. She took a step toward me and glanced at the condom display. "Is there something else I can help you with, young man?" But her eyes said, *Don't I know your mother?*

I grabbed some Gatorade and got out of there.

The next day, I went back at a different time, hoping to find a different set of employees working. I didn't see Miss Reading Glasses anywhere, but I still couldn't bring myself to get what I needed. I came away with toothpaste, a pair of socks, a box of toothpicks, and something that would relieve temporary itching of hemorrhoidal tissue.

"I can't believe you didn't get them," Tuck said.

"No, but if you ever have hemorrhoid problems, I'm your man."

Tuck had borrowed his dad's SUV, and as we drove to pick up our dates, I couldn't help noticing the size of the back seat. If this girl from out of state really wanted to get to know me, there was room for it to happen.

Tuck reached for his Skoal can and offered me a mint. "Just in case you have lizard breath," he said. "And remember, look her in the eye when you speak to her."

Dang, he wanted me to talk?

"I'm good at eye contact," I told him.

"I know you, Elroy. You tend to drop your eyes and keep them there."

"That's Vern. I'll keep my eyes where they're supposed to be." At least I'd try.

The closer we got to his girlfriend's house, the more nervous I became. I'd spent most of the year trying to get past first base, but what if she wanted a home run?

Tuck sensed what I was feeling. Maybe because I was sweating while the air conditioner was on. "Relax, man," he said. "It's like I always tell you guys—just be friendly. Expect nothing in return."

"And look her in the eye?"

"Yes." As we turned onto his girlfriend's street, I began to imagine my blind date. Would she be Shamu or something a little more delicate? I'd hate to get squashed by someone I hardly knew.

When Tuck pulled into the driveway, both girls were sitting on the front steps, and my jaw dropped. It was like Marisa had two sisters, both dark-haired, both stunning. They had on jeans and sweaters that left little to the imagination. Tuck reached over and lifted my chin to shut my mouth. "Stop drooling."

"I'm trying," I said. "Which one's my date?"

"Does it matter?"

He had a point. How do you decide between beautiful and gorgeous? We parked and got out and walked over to the girls. Tuck yanked off his John Deere hat and bowed. "Ladies." Then he turned to me. "This is Elroy. Elroy, meet Cindy and Rachel."

I shook their hands, not letting my eyes wander. They really, really wanted to, but I forced them to behave. "Nice to meet you," I said.

Cindy kissed Tuck on the lips. Either she was extremely friendly or Rachel was my date for the evening. I guessed it was the latter. This was confirmed a few minutes later, when she got in the back seat with me. We headed across town to Santino's, best pizza on the West Coast. Or at least West Highmont Ridge.

The place was pretty packed. I thought I saw a few Second Base Club members. And I noticed a few jaws drop. Yes, gentlemen, I may not be a member of your organization, but the hottest girl in the room is with me. At least, she was in the top two.

We took a booth near the back, and I promptly forgot about the Second Base Club. I was on the verge of getting there myself. I was thigh to thigh with Rachel from—

"Where did you say you're from?" I asked her.

"Atlanta," she said. "Y'all from California have such cute accents."

"I don't know about accents," Tuck said, "but we are cute."

Our pizza came, and we ate and talked, and I was part of it all. I initiated conversation. I told jokes. And I kept getting looks from Tuck, as if he was saying, *Who are you and what have you done with Elroy?* He also gave me little gestures to tell me when my eyes were wandering.

It was a good time. After a while, I forgot that I was thigh to thigh with a hot girl. Okay, maybe I didn't forget, but I was enjoying myself.

By the time we finished the meal, it was dark. We got back in the SUV, and Tuck said, "So—you guys want to go for a drive?" Which meant, *Do you* girls *want to go park?*

"The night's young," Cindy said.

"And so are we," Rachel added.

Let me just say that at this point I was thanking my lucky stars. I was full of hope and good ol' American horniness. Tuck drove through town, then turned off on a road that took us up into the hills. If you were going to park, you might as well have a view. The road turned to dirt after a while, and we kept climbing. This eventually led us to a chain-link fence with a locked gate.

"Be back in a second," Tuck said and got out, leaving the car running.

I got out and followed. At the gate, Tuck pulled out a key and inserted it into a padlock, which was connected to a chain. "Got a friend who works in the oil fields." He gestured to the oil pumps beyond the fence, bobbing up and down like feeding horses.

I nodded and helped him swing the gate open, then turned back to the SUV. "Wait." Tuck grabbed me by the shoulder and shoved something into my back pocket. "Protection," he said. "This is your night, Elroy."

I could feel myself starting to sweat again. I knew what was coming—or at least I had a hunch.

"Just go with it," Tuck said. "Be friendly, no expectations."

We got back into the SUV and drove through the gates and parked in a small turnout in the dirt road. Tuck got out and went around to the rear of the vehicle, opened the door, and grabbed a blanket. "Come on, Cindy," he said. "Let's give these two some privacy."

Yikes!

The rear doors closed, Cindy got out, and Rachel and I were alone. I kept my eyes straight ahead at first, but I could feel her eyes on me, and her perfume was doing a number on my nose. My smoothness and confidence from dinner vanished. I was no longer Super Elroy—it was just me. I turned to her and said, "So . . . uh . . . Rachel, tell me about—"

She put a finger to my lips and leaned in and kissed me. A tiny peck at first, but then her lips parted, and so did mine. We kissed again. This time deeper—it went on and on. I wanted to glance at my watch but I didn't. I just went with it, as Tuck had suggested. Just be friendly? Well, okay. Kissing was friendly, right?

I ran my hand up and down her side as we kissed, and that's when I realized something. My forearm was touching her breast. I was halfway to second base! The forearm is connected to the wrist, which is connected to the hand. I adjusted slightly so that my wrist was where my forearm had been. I opened one eye to check that her eyes were still closed. They were. She was into it. I thought I heard her moan. Or maybe that was me. We kept kissing, passionately kissing. And then—

I went for it. All the way to second base.

She broke off the kiss and pushed me away. "Okay, down, boy."

I glanced at my crotch. Too late. I pushed against her outstretched arms and began fumbling with the top button on her sweater.

"Elroy, I said stop!"

My ears weren't hearing. I kept fiddling with the button.

"Elroy!"

The button came off in my hand. *Oh, crap.* It was ornamental. The sweater was a pullover. I looked up just in time to catch her hand across my face. *SLAP!* Only it wasn't a slap. It was her fist. Her ring dug into my cheek.

"You ripped my sweater," she said. "I told you to stop."

"Sorry," I said. "I didn't hear." I didn't *want* to hear, was more like it.

She moved as far away from me as she could, as if I was some kind of leper. I sat there feeling stupid, stroking my cheek. Neither of us spoke. We were stranded until Tuck got back to take us home. After a while, I couldn't take the silence and got out of the car. "Sorry, Rachel. I'm an asshole."

"Yes, you are."

I stood by the car and looked down at the lights of Highmont Ridge. I could be cruising Thompson with Vern in the Trap. Instead, I was being a jerk with a girl I hardly knew. An hour later, Tuck and Cindy showed up. The look on my face must have said it all.

Tuck just shook his head sadly. "Get in, Elroy," he said. "I'll take you home."

CHAPTER TWENTY-NINE

Mom was up reading when I got back to the Airstream. "How'd it go?" she asked, looking up from her magazine.

"I'm kind of tired," I told her. "Mind if we talk about this tomorrow?"

"No problem." But she didn't get up. Either she figured I'd eventually spill the beans if she lingered long enough, or she forgot that the couch she was sitting on doubled as my bed.

I stood there waiting. Then I pointed. "That's where I sleep."

"Oh, right." She jumped up and went to the kitchen and started doing something in the sink.

"I like the lights out when I sleep," I said. "We'll talk tomorrow, Mom. I promise."

"Fair enough." She turned out the kitchen light and headed down the hall to her bedroom.

The next day, I still wasn't in the mood for conversation. I could see her staring at the scratch on my cheek from Rachel's ring. But I wasn't talking. At least not about the blind date.

Over breakfast I asked, "Do monks really have to take a vow of poverty?"

"Are you giving up on girls already? You're only sixteen."

"Keeping my options open," I told her. "But solitude is sounding pretty good right now."

That's all I was saying. She knew something hadn't gone right on the date. She didn't have to know the details. After breakfast, I went out back and hung on my pull-up branch for a while, but couldn't bring myself to do one. Finally, I dropped to the ground and headed into the canyon. I forced the events of the previous night to the back of my brain—a long hike might do me good.

That night at Ernesto's, it was less busy than I would have liked.

"Did you take up boxing?" Juana Maria had a nose for details, and right now she was nosing about my cheek. I still wasn't in the mood for conversation.

"Don't ask," I said.

"Well, I'm asking. What are friends for?"

"I'll tell you later," I told her.

"Did you get in a fight or something? If so, did you win? What's the other guy look like? Was it over a girl? Speak, Elroy."

A customer walked in and saved me from spilling the story. Juana Maria was a little better at getting me to talk than my mother, or almost getting me to. But I wasn't ready yet. The memory was too fresh.

Back at school, I went about my business. I was glad to be there. I needed something to focus on, something to keep my mind from thinking. Which is kind of weird, if you ponder that one. Isn't school a place you go *to* think? It did give me some welcome mental distraction, though. For a while.

Sampson Teague, who wouldn't get my vote as the world's most sensitive person, noticed my post–punch-in-the-face funk. I was in the middle of a set of curls when he said, "What's her name?"

"Excuse me?" I put the weights down and looked at him.

"It's gotta be about a girl. It's written all over your face. That's girl torment if I ever saw it."

I nodded. "See this mark on my cheek?" I asked.

He leaned in close for a look and whistled. "Nice one."

"I guess you could say I forced my attentions on a young lady who didn't appreciate it."

Sampson took another look at my cheek and nodded. "She does good work."

After class we headed back to the locker room together and Sampson put a hand on my shoulder. "You know, Elroy, not all girls are like that."

"Like what?"

He pointed to my cheek. "Like that. Some girls are . . . nicer. I'm part of an organization here at school. We put on parties. Lots of girls show up. Friendly girls." He punched me lightly on the shoulder. "Know what I'm saying? Friendly girls. We're having a party this Friday and you, Elroy, are invited."

"Not everyone in your"—I made quotation marks— " 'organization' likes me." In fact, I was pretty sure that a certain oversized hairy fellow hated my guts.

"There are a few jerks, but you'll be my guest. If anyone bothers you, I'll take care of him."

"I don't know."

"It's always a good time. You should come."

"I'll think about it," I said.

An invitation to a Second Base Club party. How do you like

that? Sampson kept bringing it up throughout the week. "Friendly girls," he kept saying. "You'll have a great time." I didn't give him an answer, but I was leaning toward saying yes. In the meantime, I spent a few nights at Ernesto's.

"Your boxing injury is looking better," Juana Maria said. "Looks more like a cat fight now." She meowed and made her fingers into claws.

I touched the side of my face. The wound was healing, and I was slowly getting back to normal, mentally. Rachel was probably back in Atlanta by now. I forced myself to think of something else.

"So how was your spring break?" I asked her. Spring break was a while ago, but I had to talk about something.

"You mean Easter vacation? I go to Aquinas. We don't call it spring break."

"So how was it?"

"Awesome." She held her arms out to the sides and spun around. "Like my tan? I spent the week at the beach."

It was a great tan. In fact, it was a great everything. It's not often that a girl *asks* to be checked out. I gave her a brief but thorough examination.

"Not bad." I spun around. "Like my freckles? I spent the week in the mountains." Actually, it was a few days.

She told me she loved my freckles. According to her, I had the most adorable freckles.

I fought back a blush and lost. There's only so much hot-girl attention a guy can take. I stared at my arm. "Really?"

"Yep, and you know what else?"

"You're a big fan of warts?"

She shook her head. "You rocked at Battle of the Bands. I liked your music a lot."

Wow. Cute *and* with good taste. What more could a guy ask for? Juana Maria looked up at me and smiled, and my heart skipped a beat. Or two.

I forced myself to say something. "Uh . . . I thought you liked country? Shania Twang."

"I like rock too. When are you playing again?"

"Not sure. We haven't played at all since I was tomatoed onstage."

"That guy was an asshole!"

I shot her a look. "Juana Maria."

"Oops. Did I say that out loud?" She laughed. "But he was. Some of the crowd liked your song, and I was one of them. I wanted to hear more."

I imagined myself onstage playing music with this pretty Mexican girl in the audience, watching my every move. Kind of a hot thought, actually.

"Thanks," I said. I gave her a hug and held her a second longer than necessary. I don't think she minded.

We got busy seating customers and making salads. It didn't start slowing down until after nine-thirty, and we finished our shift wrapping silverware for the next day.

"Are you busy Friday night?" Juana Maria asked.

"Friday?"

"Yeah. My little sister is turning seven. We're having a party for her. I'd like you to come, if you're not doing anything."

I flashed on her so-called psycho father and his baseball bat.

The Second Base Club party was on Friday. Let me think, watch a seven-year-old unwrap gifts or hang out with some "friendly" girls. Hmm . . . what to do?

Juana Maria poked me with a finger. "So—what do you say?"

"Sorry, Juana Maria, I'm busy that night. Rain check?"

"Absolutely." But she had a look in her eye. A hurt look.

I was a jerk, okay? But I couldn't stop myself. I had to go to the Second Base Club party. I'd watched them from a distance all year. Sampson had asked me, and I couldn't take that lightly. Still, in the back of my mind I knew I was making a mistake. And I'd hurt a good friend in the process. I was such a fool.

The next day, at weight training, I told Sampson that I was in.

"Excellent," he said. "I'm telling you, Elroy, trust me on this—you'll have a good time."

We worked through our circuit in record time. Coach was so impressed that he sent us to the showers early. Then we headed to the parking lot.

"You need a ride home?" Sampson asked.

Vern and the Trap had always been my ride home, but I found myself nodding. "Sure." It was strange being included as part of the in crowd. We got into his car, which was a late-model Mustang, and headed out of the parking lot. We passed Vern on the way. He was standing near the Trap, looking at me with his hands raised: *What gives?*

I had no idea. Here I was invited to an in-crowder party and being driven around by the head in-crowder. How had I gotten here? I didn't know, and I wasn't sure I wanted to analyze the hell out of it. Just go with the flow, I told myself. It had worked before.

But something was nagging me, something hard to ignore. True, I was hanging with the head in-crowder, but I'd hurt two people to get there. Two friends. Two very good friends.

On Friday, I started getting ready for the party fairly early. I took an extra-long shower, ignoring my mother pounding on the door to remind me about our small septic tank. Then I shaved the few visible whiskers on my face and splashed on aftershave, some-thing I'd picked up at the Walgreens the day before.

I put on clean jeans and a dress shirt, the same outfit from Battle of the Bands. The tomato stain was gone, and it was wrinkle-free.

"So you're not going to join the monastery after all?" Mom asked.

"It's still an option, but . . . nah." I twirled. "How do I look?"

"Sexy." Moms should never say the word "sexy." "Hand-some," maybe. But never "sexy."

A few minutes later, we heard the roar of an engine. *Crap!* I forgot to tell Vern I'd made other plans. He pulled to a stop in front of the Airstream and got out. I opened the door.

"Ready, Elroy? Let's make like a tree and"—he gestured down the road—"you know."

"I do?"

"It's Friday, man. It's you, me, the Trap, and whatever happens, happens."

Once again, the word "jerk" flashed before my eyes. I'd ig-nored a beautiful girl who adores my freckles, and now I was about to ditch my best friend. A knot formed in my stomach.

"Vern." It was all I could say.

"Elroy."

We stood there looking at each other. Finally, I forced myself to speak. "I can't go tonight. I made other plans." But even as I said the words, it seemed ridiculous. What was wrong with me? Had I lost my mind completely?

"This has something to do with you and Sampson, doesn't it?"

I nodded. "Yeah." Keep it short, I figured. I had no reasonable argument. I was hurting a friend, plain and simple, in favor of a group of people I hardly knew.

"They're a bunch of assholes, Elroy. They're not your friends."

"Sorry, Vern," I told him. "I'm really sorry." This was true. I was sorry. I was a jerk and I was sorry. But for some reason, I just couldn't stop myself. Even as I saw the hurt in Vern's eyes, memories flashed inside my head—Marisa turning away when I tried to kiss her, Carol Ann's stiff-arm, Rachel's well-placed left hook. I had to go through with this.

"You're not one of them. You'll never be one of them."

I didn't say anything, but I knew he was right.

"Vern," I said again, at a loss to say more.

He shook his head. "Whatever, man." He got into the car and drove away, his middle finger extended out the window.

I shut the Airstream door and turned around to face my mother, who was standing there with her arms folded across her chest. "Is there something you want to tell me?" she asked.

What could I say? She saw what had happened. I'd just rejected my best friend in favor of a guy I didn't know all that well.

"Elroy, what's going on?" Mom asked.

"Nothing, Mom. Everything's fine." But I knew I was lying even as I said the words. There was nothing fine about it. Treating a friend like shit was never fine.

CHAPTER THIRTY

A few minutes later, I heard tires crunching on the gravel in front of the Airstream. Unlike the Trap, Sampson's car didn't give you an audio alert from a mile away. I opened the door.

Sampson called out the window, "You ready?"

"Yeah," I said. Then I turned to my mom to tell her good-bye. She was standing behind me, peering over my shoulder.

"Who's your friend?" she asked.

"Sampson. Gotta go, Mom. I'll see you later."

"I'd like to meet him, Elroy." She gave me her I'm-your-mother-and-what-are-you-up-to? look.

I wasn't sure what I was up to. Hurting the people I cared about? The image of Vern's extended middle finger kept playing in my head. I knew this was the wrong choice. But I'd already gone too far. I couldn't go back now.

I waved Sampson over. He shut off the engine and stepped out of the car. I think I heard my mother catch her breath. She wasn't used to my hanging out with the stud muffin of the school.

Her eyes kept flicking from me to Sampson and back, like we were the oddest pairing she'd ever seen.

"Mom, this is Sampson Teague," I said.

"Hello," she said.

Sampson extended his hand. "Any mom of Elroy's is a mom of mine." When she didn't laugh he added, "It's nice to meet you."

It was pretty hard not to be charmed by the guy, but I could tell my mother was resisting.

"We won't be too late," I said, jumping off the porch and heading to the car. I wanted to get out of there before she imposed a curfew. I didn't know who these friendly girls were, but it might take most of the night to find out. "Bye, Mom."

We got in the car and took off down Casitas Pass.

"Your mom's nice," Sampson said. "She's also hot. Really hot. Extremely—"

"You can stop now. She's my mother."

"Oh, yeah, sorry."

We drove north of town along the 101 and pulled off onto some kind of private driveway. I didn't ask any questions, but kept wondering, What is it about going up into the hills when you want to get lucky? I checked out the terrain. There were no oil pumps, just acres and acres of citrus, a barn in the distance. We pulled in front of a huge ranch house surrounded by about thirty cars. Loud music played, and I heard laughter.

The party was in full swing, all in-crowders, and I was invited.

I held out my arm to Sampson as he put the car in park. "Go ahead," I told him.

"Go ahead what?"

"Pinch me."

He laughed. "Expect the time of your life, Elroy."

"If you say so."

We got out and walked toward the entrance. One of the football players—probably a lineman, from the size of him—was standing out front beside a couple of ice chests full of beer. "Hold up, you two." He tossed us a few beers. "You know the drill."

I looked at the beer in my hand, then at Sampson. "The drill?"

"Gotta down a beer before you join the party. Kind of an entry fee."

He cracked his open, and so did I. I sipped while Sampson guzzled. Then he crushed the can against his forehead and flipped it onto a pile of empties. I drank mine at my own pace while Sampson stood there tapping his foot. What can I say? I'm a wimpy drinker. When I finished, I dropped my can on the ground and crushed it with my foot. Pointing to my forehead, I said, "I may need to use this later on."

Sampson and I went inside the house. The whole place seemed to vibrate with the loudness of the music, and it smelled like beer. People were everywhere, standing in groups, flopped on couches, a few couples making out. Yes, there were lots of girls. And they looked pretty friendly.

Somebody yelled, "Sampson!" Suddenly he was surrounded, and since I was standing near him, so was I.

"What's he doing here?" I turned and saw Hairy Jerry looking right at me. He seemed bigger than the last time I saw him. And he smelled of alcohol.

"Elroy is my guest, Jerry," Sampson said. "Do you have a problem with that?"

"He's not a member," Jerry said, not taking his eyes off me.

"I invited him." Sampson stepped between me and Jerry. "Is there a problem?"

No answer. Just the two of them standing eyeball to eyeball. Finally, Jerry turned around and walked away. "Whatever, man."

I pulled Sampson to the side. "I shouldn't have come. Jerry's right. I don't belong here."

"Nonsense. Who died and left him in charge?" He gestured around the room. "There are a few jerks, but most of the people here are nice." He nudged me with an elbow. "Especially the girls, Elroy. Go mingle. Talk to somebody."

"Where are you going?"

"I'll be around," he said, and disappeared into the crowd.

Great. I was just abandoned by the guy who'd invited me. I scanned the room. Sampson had joined a group of girls dancing together. Jerry was on the other side of the room, giving me his death stare. I looked away. And that's when I saw a familiar face.

"Carol Ann!"

"Hey, Elroy. How's it going?" She was in jeans and a fairly snug top. More makeup than usual. She still wasn't a Marisa, but she was making a decent attempt at it.

"Pretty good," I said. If ditching your best friend only to be ditched yourself could be considered good. "Have you been to one of these parties before?"

"Nope. First time." She shrugged and looked around the room. "Looks like fun."

"Yeah, we'll see."

"Nice to see you, Elroy." She was about to move on.

"Sorry about the backwards dance," I blurted out.

"No problem. I still had a good time. Just didn't want to . . . you know."

Yeah, I knew. That stiff-arm to my Adam's apple was some kind of hint.

She gave me a wave and wandered off. I knew two people

in a party of a hundred. It was a start, I figured. I meandered past a bunch of dancing bodies, Sampson no longer among them, and made my way into the kitchen. A beer keg sat in a huge container of ice. A Second Base Club member was filling cups and handing them to people, whether they wanted them or not.

I wasn't much of a drinker but soon found myself holding a cup of beer. Oh well, I figured, taking a swig. If I was going to be expected to talk with the opposite sex, I needed to shed a few inhibitions.

"Bottoms up," I said. Someone walking by banged cups with me, and I took another long drink. I wasn't feeling anything yet, but it was just a matter of time before Elroy the introvert morphed into Elroy the extrovert.

A few minutes later, Sampson showed up. He held up two fingers. "Two, please."

The guy pouring the drinks gave him two, then dropped something into one of them. "Right hand," he said with a wink.

"Got it," Sampson said, and went back into the living room.

I stood there staring at the spot where Sampson had been standing. Did I just see what I thought I saw? A little white pill dropped into one of the drinks? I tried to get my mind around the thought. *Was that what the Second Base Club was all about? Scoring with girls because they couldn't say no?*

The guy pouring drinks saw my confusion and said, "Just stacking the deck in our favor, if you know what I mean."

Stacking the deck? Holy crap!

I had to get out of there. Vern had said it best—I wasn't one of them and I never would be. And now I knew I didn't want to be. It was time to leave. But I was miles from Highmont, and my ride was in serious seduction mode.

I felt for my cell phone. Damn. My pockets were empty. In

my rush to get away before my mom imposed a curfew, I'd left my phone behind.

I went back into the living room. It was more crowded than before, and new arrivals were still coming through the front entrance. The dance floor had expanded, with more guys joining in. And everywhere I looked I saw cups of beer. How many had been enhanced? I wondered.

I had to find Sampson. Maybe I could snap him out of seduction mode long enough to get him to drive me home. There was a hall leading away from the main room. I followed it to another large room, where a few guys were shooting pool and a couple more were lounging on couches. Sampson was there, heading outside through a set of sliding glass doors on the far side of the room.

He was not alone. Carol Ann was with him.

Chapter Thirty-One

"**H**ey, Sampson."

He didn't hear me. He'd already gone out and shut the door.

I had started across the room when one of the guys playing pool stood up, blocking my path.

"Looks like your protection has left the building."

It was Hairy Jerry. The guy wasn't just extra large, he was gigantic, and he was right. With Sampson gone, there was no one around to keep me from being pounded on. I tried to scoot past him, but he was surprisingly light on his feet.

"Where you going, man?" he said.

"I gotta talk to Sampson."

"Sorry, he's not around." Jerry moved closer. I could smell the beer on his breath, and my heart lurched. "Tell you what"—he gestured to a pool table—"if you beat me in a game of pool, I won't kick your ass. How does that sound?"

He put his huge hand around my neck and pulled me into the room, placing a cue stick in my hand. "Sound like a deal?"

"Do I have a choice?" I asked.

"Not really."

The guy he'd been playing with laughed. So did a few others. They were all looking forward to seeing a double ass-kicking, in billiards and blood.

"I suck at pool," I said.

"That makes one of us," Jerry said. "Tell you what, I'll let you break."

I looked around at his cronies, who were still drooling in anticipation, and shook my head. "Nah, you break."

I waited for Jerry to walk around to the far side of the table, then I bolted back down the hallway toward the party. Maybe there was safety in numbers. I jog-danced across the dance floor and ducked into the kitchen.

"Slow down," one of the keg guys said, placing another beer in my hands.

Most of it sloshed onto the floor as I kept moving. I went out the kitchen door and tossed the beer aside. Now to find Sampson. I ran around the side of the house to the backyard, glancing behind me. No sign of Jerry. I hoped he'd moved on to other prey, or maybe was just too drunk to travel at more than a walking pace.

A huge lawn spread out before me. "Sampson!" I yelled. There was no sign of him. I ran to the back of the yard, which was lined with lemon trees. I cut between them and found myself on a dirt path that seemed to separate lemon trees from orange trees. Far ahead of me I could see two people walking. Sampson and Carol Ann, I figured. They were heading toward the barn.

"Hey!" I called. They didn't turn around.

I went after them, closing fast, until I was able to make out their voices.

Sampson smacked cups with Carol Ann. "Let the party begin. Cheers."

She raised the cup to her lips.

"Don't, Carol Ann," I yelled, moving closer.

They turned and faced me. Sampson said, "Elroy, I'm kind of busy here, if you know what I mean."

"Yeah," I said. "I know what you mean." I looked at Carol Ann. "You don't want to do this, trust me."

"Do what?" she said.

"Do what?" Sampson repeated. "Conversation not allowed where you come from?"

Carol Ann laughed and Sampson joined her. They were laughing at me.

"You know what I'm talking about, Sampson." I pointed to Carol Ann's cup. "Do you want to tell her, or would you like me to?"

Sampson dropped the blanket he'd been holding and took a step toward me. "I invited you to this party, and this is how you repay me?" There was just enough moonlight for me to catch the glare in his eye. "Go back to the party, Elroy." He took another step.

But there was no stopping me. All year I'd looked up to the Second Base Club. But no more. Someone had to expose them for what they really were.

"Have you told her about your little secret organization, Sampson? The Second Base Club? Have you told her about the scoring system?" When he didn't answer I said, "He put something in your drink, Carol Ann."

"What?"

"Don't listen to him, Carol Ann. Your drink is fine." He glowered at me. "And Elroy was just leaving."

He put his arm around her, and they turned away from me.

I'd be leaving soon, but not yet. "Wait!" I said. I moved forward and knocked the cup out of Carol Ann's hand, spilling it on the ground. "You two have a good evening."

My job was finished here. I'd find a ride home with someone else.

"That does it." Sampson threw his drink aside and took a swing at me. I was just out of reach. He tried again, but I dodged it. One more try . . . and then I shot in on him, caught him clean in a double-leg takedown. He went down, and I landed on top of him. I brought my fist back to finish the job and—

A large hand grabbed me from behind, yanking me to my feet. I knew it was Jerry even before I turned and saw him, before I smelled his beer breath, before his fist connected with my jaw and sent me sprawling into the dirt. I sat up slowly, trying to clear my head. Sampson was sitting beside me, dusting himself off.

"He knows everything, Sampson."

"Yeah, I heard."

Carol Ann had her phone out. She dialed three numbers, then yelled for help and blurted out the location of the party. Jerry turned and smacked the phone from her hand.

"Get back to the house, Carol Ann," I said.

"Yes," Jerry agreed, both fists clenched. "Unless you want to see Elroy bleed."

I got to my feet and went in low against Jerry, expecting him to go down like Sampson. But he was a brick wall. He tossed me to the side like I was a preschooler and came at me, cocking a fist. My heart jackhammered. Another shot at a take-down wouldn't work against this guy. I had to find a different way, and fast.

Jerry turned his head toward Carol Ann. "Seriously. You don't want to see this," he told her.

I saw my chance. I was still on the ground, Jerry's knee level with my eyes. Knees bend only one way, right? I mule-kicked as hard as I could. His knee gave, and he fell, howling in pain.

"Let's get out of here," I yelled. I jumped to my feet, grabbed Carol Ann's hand, and ran into the orchard.

We raced through the trees, stumbling over roots and the occasional dark object in the night. I had no plan other than putting some distance between us and the Second Base Club.

After a while, we came to a low rock wall. We scrambled over it and looked back.

"Are you okay?" I asked, breathing hard.

She nodded. "So far." I could see the fear in her eyes as we scanned the orchard and listened.

"There." She pointed. Two figures were coming toward us, the bigger one limping and holding something.

I turned to Carol Ann. "Get back to the house. They want me, not you."

"What if they see me?"

"I'll distract them. Get back to the house and get help."

She nodded and began moving along the wall to the left. When she was maybe thirty yards away, I stood up. "Hey, dick-wads! You want a piece of me?"

I stood my ground until I was sure Sampson and Jerry had locked in on me. Then I ran, following the wall to the right. When the wall ended, I darted through a small patch of trees that opened into a clearing in front of the barn. One of the doors was ajar.

I sprinted across the clearing and went inside, closing the door behind me.

I didn't have time to wait for my eyes to adjust to the lack of light. No telling how close Sampson and Jerry were. I banged my shin on some kind of farm vehicle and felt my way around it to the back. Not the best hiding place, but at least I was out of sight.

I squatted and waited, massaging my shin.

Minutes clicked by. I was about to move out from behind the vehicle when the door swung open. I flattened myself on the dirt floor of the barn, my heart pounding. Beneath the vehicle I could make out a pair of legs. Just one pair.

"Elroy, it's Sampson."

I didn't move a muscle, barely breathed.

"This is ridiculous. Let's get you back to the house, call it a night. Jerry's a psycho. You'll be safe with me."

I wanted nothing more than to call it a night. But could I trust Sampson, now that I knew the truth? And now that he knew I knew?

"Come on, Elroy. Don't make me look for you. Let's get out of here. I'll take you home."

I stayed quiet. Was Sampson out to get me, or was he just a horny teenager who'd temporarily lost his way?

"Elroy."

I believed it was the latter. He was a fool, not a psycho.

"I'm here," I said. I stood up and stepped out from behind what I now realized was a tractor.

"It's okay," Sampson said. "Jerry's gone. He's probably passed out someplace, sleeping it off."

But what if he's lying? I told myself. We faced off on opposite sides of the tractor. The longer I stood there, the more I understood that this was just Sampson, the guy I lifted weights with, and something told me to trust him.

"You really did a number on his knee."

"I had to," I said, moving forward. I could feel my heartbeat getting back to normal.

"Yeah, like I said, Jerry's not quite right in the head. Let's get out of here."

"Sounds good," I said. I kept walking toward him.

When we were face to face, he smiled, then gestured to the door. "Brains before beauty."

"You first," I said. "Age before brains."

"No problem."

Sampson stepped through the doorway, and I followed.

But someone was there waiting for me. The two-by-four was in motion before I could even think of ducking. I caught a glimpse of Jerry's snarl, then felt the wood crash against my skull, and I went down, Jerry standing over me. I tried to stay conscious, but I could feel myself slipping away. Strange lights flashed against the side of the barn.

"Hold it right there," said a loud voice.

Then everything went black.

Chapter Thirty-Two

I woke up with my mom's face about an inch from mine.

"Can you hear me, Elroy?"

"I can hear you, Mom. I can also see you. But you're a little blurry. Can you back up?"

She did, and I saw that Dad was standing behind her.

I looked around. "Where am I?"

"Highmont Community." My mother's eyes were full of tears. "We're so proud of you, honey."

They filled me in on what occurred after Jerry took a two-by-four to my skull. Apparently, Carol Ann made it back to the party and got help. But it was the 911 call she'd made with her cell phone that brought the police. The ambulance came and whisked me away. The police grabbed Jerry, who was still standing over me holding his weapon of choice when they arrived.

"How long am I in for?" I asked.

"Until tomorrow," my dad said, "maybe the day after. Looks

like there's no internal bleeding or brain damage. They just want to watch you for a while to make sure."

Mom was starting to get teary again, and I looked away.

Vern showed up a while later. "Hey," he said. "How's the noggin?"

"Only hurts when I'm conscious."

He laughed. I did too, but it hurt too much, so I stopped.

"Don't say anything funny," I told him. I pointed to my head. "I can't handle it." I gestured to a chair by the window. "Take a load off."

When he did I said, "I'm so sorry, Vern. I was such a jerk."

He nodded. "Yeah, you were. But you're also my best friend. Friends forgive each other."

What a guy. I'd completely rejected him, and he was ready to take me back. Vern was a true friend. Somehow I knew I'd never take that lightly, ever again.

"Thanks, man. Chalk it up to temporary insanity."

"Yeah, kind of a high price to pay for second base."

I nodded. "Talk about getting some sense knocked into me." My head throbbed, but the rest of me felt good. It was nice to be back where I belonged.

After a while, Vern got up to leave. He held his fist out for me to bash.

"You're a good friend, Vern," I told him.

He told me not to flirt with the nursing staff, and was gone.

Mom and Dad left also, but said they'd be back bright and early in the morning.

"We're so proud of you," Mom said again.

I loved hearing that. "I should get my head bashed in more often."

"Don't you dare."

"Kidding. See you guys tomorrow."

After they left, I closed my eyes and drifted off.

I felt a cold hand against my cheek and opened my eyes.

"So, Elroy, I understand chivalry is not dead." Juana Maria was in civilian clothes, jeans and a light-blue jacket, hair down around her shoulders.

"Chivalry or stupidity. Not sure which."

"It was totally chivalrous. But, frankly, I'd expect nothing less from a rock star. What was the name of your band again? Lonesome Highway?"

"*Templin* Highway."

"That's right." She smiled, and even in my weakened state I was semi-dazzled.

She plopped herself in the chair next to the bed.

"Seriously, Juana Maria, it was nothing."

She shook her head. "I'm sure there's a girl out there who'd disagree with you. I know I do." She opened her purse and pulled out an iPod. "I brought you something."

"Please don't tell me it's country music."

"Just listen and keep an open mind." She fitted the ear buds in my ears. "Talk about a captive audience."

"No fair. Nurse, help."

"Shhhh! Listen, Elroy." She pressed "play," and suddenly my head was filled with music—acoustic guitar, mandolin, and bass. Nothing electric, no percussion.

I looked at her.

"It's bluegrass," she said.

The song ended, and I pulled out the buds. "I'm not a fan yet, but that wasn't bad."

"Want to hear another one?"

"Sure." This time she gave me one ear bud while she listened to the other.

And so it went. For more than an hour, we sat there in the hospital room listening to music, mostly her faves, but some of mine as well, and I couldn't help thinking how comfortable it was to be with her. Juana Maria had me pegged long ago when she asked, "Don't you think it's exhausting . . . being someone other than yourself?"

It was very exhausting. It was also hazardous to my health.

I looked at the girl beside me now. She wasn't my girlfriend. She was a girl who was my friend. And I began to hope for more. I did have adorable freckles, after all.

"How was the birthday party?"

"Great. You should have seen her, Elroy. She was so cute."

"I'll try to make the next one," I told her.

"I'll hold you to that." She grabbed her purse and got ready to leave.

"Wait," I said.

"Yes?"

"So what does a guy have to do to get your phone number?"

"It's a very complicated procedure. You ask for it."

"Ernesto said your dad has a baseball bat and he's not afraid to use it."

"He's a bit overprotective." She twirled. "But, Elroy, aren't I worth it?"

She was. She was totally worth it.

Wait an hour before you call her, I told myself after she left. I made it half that long.

I dialed her number. "Did you miss me?" I asked.

"I did. What took you so long?"

"Just clueless, I guess." Eight months of cluelessness, I thought.

When they let me out of the hospital, I borrowed my mom's car and drove to the mall. I found a toy store and picked out the perfect gift for a seven-year-old girl. Then I drove over to Juana Maria's to deliver it.

Juana Maria laughed. "The way to a girl's heart is through her little sister? Is that it?"

"That's it exactly."

EPILOGUE

N o one came forward to press charges. I guess, with all the drinking going on at the Second Base Club parties, inhibitions were being tossed out the window, even without the drugs. Lots of meetings took place between parents and Highmont Ridge High School staff. They made sure the Second Base Club was disbanded permanently, and in the end, no one saw any jail time, not even Hairy Jerry. The judge ruled that since it was the first time Jerry had taken a two-by-four to the skull of another human being, he wouldn't go to jail. He did, however, get a gazillion hours of community service.

This drove my parents crazy at first, but they soon found other things to occupy their time. They were going into business together, opening a yoga studio and shop in a vacant storefront on Thompson. Dad would run the shop, and Mom would teach yoga classes. The empty rectangle on my father's whiteboard finally had a purpose. Somehow I knew they'd make it work.

"What gave you the idea for the yoga studio?" I asked once.

Dad said it was all that time they'd spent watching me wrestle, at the dual meets and the all-day tournaments. In between the action on the mat, they'd had time to talk. That was what I'd liked best about my wrestling season. Even though I'd lost half of my matches, seeing Mom and Dad together a few times a week made it worth the struggle—and the mat burns.

I still lived with my mom in the trailer at the end of Casitas Pass, but there was hope. "You two look good together," I told them at every opportunity. It wasn't a lie. They did look good together. The question was, could they be good together outside of work? I was keeping my fingers crossed.

I spent the rest of that spring and summer splitting my time between hanging out with Juana Maria and making music with Vern and Tuck. Our eighth song, "Is That a Two-by-Four in Your Pants or Are You Just Glad to See Me?" was quickly becoming a local favorite. I still had a soft spot in my heart for "Templin Highway," the road song. We not only played the song, but we lived it. . . .

The Trap pulled to a stop in front of the Airstream, Vern at the wheel, Tuck riding shotgun. There was no hurricane rumbling up the canyon to announce their arrival. No blaring engine noise.

"I can't believe it." I looked at Vern. "What'd you do to it?"

Vern smiled. "New muffler."

It made a huge difference. We could hear the stereo without blasting it.

I grabbed my gear and got in. Tuck climbed in the back with no argument. Ever since my head injury, he'd been offering me the front seat. He rapped gently on the top of my skull. "Takes a lickin' and keeps on tickin'."

We all laughed, and Vern cranked up the stereo.

We were on our way to the Eastern Sierra again, one of three trips we had planned for that summer. The weather was a perfect seventy-five degrees, a light breeze blowing off the ocean, and we were heading east on the 126.

"Uh-oh," I said, pointing. "Is that who I think it is?"

"Yep," Vern and Tuck said in unison.

It was a shirtless Hairy Jerry, picking up trash along the highway.

"Vern, get in the right lane. Slow down."

Vern moved over and slowed way down. And I did what needed to be done.

I came . . . I saw . . . I mooned him.